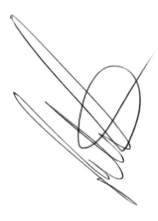

<u>Acknowledgements</u>

I would to thank the following people for

their support :

Ann B

Bev F

Cheryl P

Jane & Nigel P G

You all have either helped me or nagged me

to finish this book

Dedication

I would like to dedicate this book to my

parents

Sidney C Whitmore (1932 -)

And

Patricia A Whitmore (1936 – 2005)

<u>1</u>

Finally, A&E was empty. It was 4.30 in the morning, the first rays of sunlight glinted through the windows as the sun came up above the hills that surrounded the hospital on the outskirts of Swindon, in the north of the county of Wiltshire.

The hospital is a fairly modern hospital by most standards, so much better than the old one it replaced. That hospital had a reputation of people feeling worse when they were discharged, then they felt when they were admitted.

Carol Mcvitie was a young single mum of one little boy called Josh, who loved her job as a Staff Nurse, in the Emergency Department, she was just coming to the end of a 22-hour day / night shift

"Carol" shouted out Sister Joan, to get Carol's attention, "I'm taking some paperwork through to Intensive care, for that patient who came in with the knife wound to his chest, then I will nip off for a quick break, can you make sure the cleaners come in and clean up the mess in the Resus room." "Sure" said Carol, "Have you got the keys to the drugs cabinet, just in case we get an emergency in?"

As Sister Joan threw over the keys she said, "Let's bloody well hope not, we've had more than enough for one night."

Carol waited until Sister Joan was out of sight; she then made her way to the drugs cabinet. Before opening it, she looked all around, the only one around was a junior doctor, sat at the desk with his head buried in his paperwork. She put the key into the lock and turned the key and opened the door, the red warning light came on, but the buzzer didn't sound as it had been busted for months now.

She reached in and grabbed a handful of diamorphine vials, placing them in her pocket. She was just about to reach in again, when one of the student nurses whose name was Joanne, came around the corner and gave Carol a quizzical look. "Just checking the drug levels, ready for the early shift.

After the night we have had. It will then be ready for the early shift, when they come in, "I thought only Sister did that" quizzed Joanne.

"Sister Joan is running around like a blue arse fly, and she asked me to check the cabinet for her," she lied. "Well nobody seems to stick to the rules around here anyway" said Joanne.

The sound of the red phone ringing caught both of their attentions; Carol quickly locked the drug's cabinet, as Joanne picked up the phone. "Swindon Resus" she said calmly, as the person spoke on the other end, Joanne was frantically writing down what they were saying, making sure she wrote down everything that was said to her.

"A 55-year-old male having a MI (Myocardial infarction / heart attack) nonresponsive 15 minutes out" Joanne said to Carol.

Carol picked up the microphone and announced, "Male trauma call 15 minutes."

Even with everybody getting one of the bays in the Resus room ready for the incoming patient. There was a feeling of calmness all around the Resus room. Everyone had their job and they went about it quietly. Within 10 minutes, everything was ready for the arrival of the patient.

Carol heard the chinking of the glass vials in her pocket, she quickly looked around making sure that no one else had heard the noise, she turned to Sister Joan and said, "Just flying to the toilet, before the patient arrives?" Sister Joan shook her head and said, "don't be too long as the patient will be here very shortly."

Carol entered the toilet, she checked to make sure nobody else was in any of the cubicles, she removed the vials from her pocket and placed them inside her bra. Thanking her good luck that today of all days, she was wearing a padded bra as nothing was noticeable from the outside. The glass felt cold against her breasts, she jumped up and down on the spot to make sure the vials wouldn't fall out. She stared into the mirror and wondered to herself how it came to all this. Stealing drugs from the hospital, a boyfriend who had already moved in with her it seemed. She had found out he was into the drugs scene, only smoking cannabis but into selling the heavy stuff. He had asked her to get him some drugs from work. Because she was already head over heels in love with him and she was sure he was in love with her, she decided to steal some, only if there was no risk of her getting caught. Plus, Josh seemed to like Ben as well.

But now a bent copper was threatening to tell her bosses what she was doing, unless she supplied 'Controlled' drugs to him as well. Ben said he would sort that problem out and she prayed he would keep his word

<u>2</u>

It had all started just over 4 months ago, when Ben was admitted into A&E after being beaten up very badly. Carol was his named nursed, when he was admitted into A&E.

As she carefully wiped away the blood from his face, Ben managed to open his badly swollen eyes slightly, after a second, he said "I must have died, because I swear I have an angel standing over me." Carol smiled back at Ben and told him to keep still as she didn't want to damage his face any further. The more of the blood she wiped away, from his face, even though it was swollen to beyond belief she found herself admiring his looks. His hair was jet black and longish and unkempt, it just added to his appeal in her eyes. She estimated his height to be just over 6 feet, she couldn't really tell as he was laid on the trolley. He was of a slim build but not skinny. As she helped him out of his blood-stained tee shirt, that's when she noticed all the tattoo's over his body, she had always wanted to have a tattoo of her little boy's name on her shoulder but was too scared of needles to go through with it. Sticking needles into other people was no problem, but when it came to someone sticking a needle into her, she turned in a petrified baby. After she had finished cleaning the top half of his body, she covered him with a hospital gown, she had just started to remove the rest of his clothing, when a police officer popped his head around the curtain, smiled at Carol and said, "Could you please put the patients clothing and shoes into this bag, handing over a large clear evidence bag, as they may need them for evidence." "Yeah no problem," she replied. Turning to Ben, she smiled saying "I will be right back, don't you go anywhere" Ben shook his head "I will be right here, I promise."

The policeman sat in the chair next to the trolley. "So, Ben" he started, "are you going to tell me who has been using your face for batting practise?" Ben mumbled incoherently. "Sorry Ben I didn't get a word of that." "I said, go to hell and leave me the fuck alone." Ben growled back. Just then Carol pulled back the curtains, "sorry Staff just wanted a quick word with your patient.

Can I have a word with you as well, if you got a minute too spare." "Sure" said Carol stepping outside of the bay. Carol noticed the police officer had moved a few bays up, so as Ben couldn't overhear she presumed. "Has the patient said anything to you about how he sustained his injuries?" he asked when she was level with him. "Sorry not a word and I think it might be a while before he can say anything legible," she said looking back down towards Ben's bay. "I will come back in the morning to see if he is more talkative then." With that he turned on his heels and left the department.

Carol went back to Bens bay, pulled the chair closer to the bed and sat down, "what was that all about?" she asked Ben. "I dunno" Ben lied, "He wanted to ask me some questions about who battered me, I guess." "Why didn't you want to answer them?" Carol asked.

"Look at the state of me and because I'm in so much pain, I just didn't want to be bothered." "What did happen to you?" she asked, Ben didn't say anything for a few minutes, so much so Carol thought he had fallen off to sleep. What Carol didn't realise was that Ben was using the time to get his lies straight. "Well" he said "I was sat on a bench in the town gardens waiting for a friend, when this group of guys came up to me demanding my phone and wallet. Refusing I went to stand up and out of the corner of my eye I saw a baseball bat being swung towards my body. The pain exploded inside of me as the bat made contact with my ribs. I crumpled to the floor and then it was just kick after kick being aimed at my head and my body, I tried to roll into the foetal position to protect myself, but the kicks just kept coming and coming, the last thing I remember is seeing this boot heading straight for my face, as it made contact, I passed out.

When I awoke, I was in the back of an ambulance with a paramedic leaning over me, shining a light into my eyes. Carol was starting to feel sorry for Ben, as she listened to his story. Little did she know that most of it was lies! The reality was Ben had picked on the wrong people to try and sell a bag of icing sugar disguised as a large bag of amphetamine to some big-time criminals from Reading. Ben is a small-time drug dealer, who likes to think he can play with the big boys in the drug world. He had come to the attention of the Swindon police on many occasions, but he always seemed to get away with the charges. Because of this Ben thought he was invincible, and that no police officer could touch him, and he would never ever do jail time.

Carol stood up, and said to Ben, "I am afraid I have to remove the rest of your clothing, she removed his training shoes and pulled down his tracksuit bottoms and underwear, something inside of her made her glance at his penis. When she looked up, she realised Ben had caught her looking. Her face went bright red, and she quickly pulled the hospital gown down to protect his dignity. "Did you like what you saw?" Ben asked cheekily. Carol stumbled with her words when she replied. "I didn't really look." With that she hurried out of the bay.

The medical staff were sat at the desk chatting about the cases that had been admitted that night, when the buzzer for the bay that Ben was in, buzzed, "Carol, it's your patient." Sister said, "Carol put down the cup of coffee that she was drinking and went over to Ben's Bay. She pulled back the curtain and asked him how she could help? "I am in so much pain now; any chance I can have some more pain killers?" "I'm not sure if you can have any more yet, but I will ask the doctor." Carol went over to where the records were kept, pulled Ben's notes, she scanned down the list of medication he had already received and at what time they had been given. After reading the records, she realised that Ben was not due for any more pain relief for at least another hour. Carol then spoke to the duty doctor to see if anything else could be given.

The doctor also read the notes and said "Sorry Carol he is going to have to wait.

After being told that he couldn't have anything else for an hour, Ben started to kick off, raising his voice, he shouted out that the doctor didn't know what he was doing, and he shouldn't have to lay there in pain and that he wanted another doctor to see him now.

Carol put her hand onto his arm and said to Ben in a soft voice "Ben, it's not that we won't, it's we can't give you any more pain relief, it's just in case you have to go to theatre tonight and we wouldn't want you overdose on pain relief and die on the table now would we, it would be a waste of a good-looking guy, even if he is covered in cuts and bruises." Carol said with a big smile on her face. Ben tried to force a smile, even though it was painful, "I'm sorry for kicking off at you," Ben said,

"You are far too beautiful to be shouted at, please will you accept my apologises, I promise not to blow again."

3

Carol continued with her shift, dealing with patients, dealing with doctors. Her feet were killing her; her back was aching like a bitch, she hadn't had time for something to eat. She wondered if it would stay the same when the new Charge Nurse Jason James, took over A&E next week. She had worked with Jason a few years ago, when she was training. He had seemed ok then, but she remembered Jason ran a very tight ship, when it came to work he was all business, Jason enjoyed a laugh when things were slack. But he was most well-known for defending his staff to the limit, when he thought they were right, he never just took a doctor's word as right. If he thought the doctor was wrong, he was not afraid about going up against any consultant, even if the consultant thought he or she was god. Thankfully there are very few doctors who have that attitude these days, but there are still some old dinosaurs around.

Just before her shift ended she was bagging up a patient's belongings, who had died suddenly. When she came across a packet of Tramadol painkillers, without really thinking about it, she slipped them into her pocket, and then finished bagging everything else up and putting the bag behind the desk. Carol made her way back to Ben's bay. "How are you feeling now?" "Shit" came the reply. She leant close to his ear and whispered "Don't ever tell anyone I gave you these, taking the box of tramadol out of her pocket, take 2 now and 2 more every 4 hours, on top of whatever the doctors give you.

Make sure you keep the tablets totally away from ANY member of staff." "Oh My God," he whispered back, "A beautiful angel and a real caring person, you Carol are the most precious person I have ever met, I think I'm in love with you already." Not only having empathy for him but there was also something about the look of him. She hadn't had any male attention for the past 18 months, which she was missing.

Carol had a smile not only on her face but in her eyes as well. She put her hand gently on his face and said, "I'm going off duty soon; I know they are going to be keeping you in for a few days, I will see if I can pop in and see how you are doing before I start my duty tomorrow morning." Somewhere in the back of his head, Ben realised he had Carol right where he wanted her. Now he would be able to use her not only just for sex, but a way into hospital supplies and drugs if he played it carefully. "I will be looking forward to that so much," he said in the softest sexiest voice he could.

Carol's shift finished, as she made her way home, she found herself thinking about Ben. The more she thought about him the more she knew she would like to know him better.

After Carol had left him, Ben picked up his phone, he scrolled through his contacts until he found who he was looking for. Making sure that no members of staff were anywhere close to him, he dialled the number, the call was answered after a few rings, "hi there Jill, it's Ben, how's it going?" "Yeah I'm good," said Jill, "What's up?" "Well some tramadol have come into my possession, and was wondering if you were in the market for any?" The voice on the other end of the phone asked how much the tablets were,

"I think a fiver each would be a good price for both of us." Jill asked how many tablets were available and Ben said he had 24 for sale, "how many would you like?" Jill said that she would take all of them. "The only problem is you will have to come up to the hospital as I am in A&E now, I will be going up to a ward shortly,

but I don't know which one yet, I'll text you when I do know. I don't want to run the risk of you coming into A&E, you know what it's like, the police are always here sniffing around trying to chat up the nurses and young female doctors. I don't want to give them a reason to come and search me if they recognise you coming into to see me."

Jill said she would wait for his text and see him later. Ben smiled as he ended the call and thought to himself, well Carol that's the first £120 you have made me. I know for a fact you are going to earn me a damn sight more before you are no longer any use to me.

As Ben lay there he thought to himself that if it was that easy to get Carol to get him pills would he be able to persuade anymore of the nurses to provide him with even more drugs?

After the doctors were satisfied they had covered all Ben's symptoms, he was transferred to the observation ward and within the hour Jill had been up to the hospital and collected the tablets, leaving Ben, to drift off to sleep.

For the rest of the night, no matter how hard he tried he could not persuade any of the other members of staff to give him extra drugs.

The next morning, Carol made sure she arrived at the hospital 45 minutes early; she logged in onto the computer in A&E and found out that Ben had been moved to the observation ward. She made her way there. She went up to the nurse's station and asked how her patient was doing, the staff nurse looking after the ward, said that Ben had been a pain in the arse all night by complaining that he was in constant pain and trying to get more and more medication. The staff nurse also said that she did not believe he was in as much pain as he was making out. Carol asked if she could pop in and see him and the staff nurse said that it wasn't a problem.

Carol looked on the admissions board to find out what bed he was in. She walked into a four bedded male ward noticing that Ben was already awake and on his phone.

Ben smiled and put his hand up when he noticed Carol coming into the ward; he muttered something into his phone and ended the call. "Hi, how are you doing?" She asked. "Yeah I'm not too bad, but I'm in so much pain."

"I was just speaking to the staff nurse at the nurse's station and she said that you were a pain in the bum all night complaining about your pain, did you not take the pills that I gave you?"

Ben's mind was going over and over trying to think of an excuse, finally he said that he had taken two, but had fallen asleep before they transferred him here to this ward, when he had awoken the tablets were nowhere to be seen, and that he did not want to ask about them just in case it got you into trouble. Aww bless him thought Carol, not wanting to get me into trouble when easily could have done. "I don't suppose you have any more pain killers?"

Ben whispered. "Sorry no I don't," she replied. Ben pulled a sad dog face which made Carol smile. I have to go on duty now, but if you want I will come and see you when I finish this afternoon? Ben reached out and took hold of her hand and said, "Nothing would make me happier." "Ok see you later," she turned and made her way back to the A&E dept., with a little skip in her step.

4

A few days later, Ben was released from the hospital, by time he got back to his dingy flat he was desperate for a fix of anything, everyone he called, either didn't have anything or didn't answer his call.

Finally, he managed to get hold of Jill the one he sold the tramadol too, "Jill I'm really hanging here, have you got anything for me?" "Yeah come on over and we'll have a party for two."

Half an hour later, Ben was sat in Jill's front room, starting to relax after popping 4 pills, swallowed down with a large glass of Vodka.

"The old bill really have been hitting the suppliers in Swindon and as far down as Bristol one way and Reading the other way" Jill said, "Where did you get those pills from?" "I got them from a girl that I have just met and with a wee bit of the old Ben charm, I'm hoping she will get me more, but stronger ones." He replied.

"Well keep me in mind when you get reloaded, and by the way the drinks free but you owe me a twenty note for the pills." Ben gave her the money and made his way back to the town centre to see what else he could get hold off.

Carol felt the phone buzz in her pocket, she reached into her pocket, unlocked the phone, and saw that she had 6 messages and 4 missed calls from Ben. Wow he is keen, she thought to herself. She opened the messages, the first asked how she was, and the second said that he had been sent home from the hospital,

the third was asking if she wanted to meet up for a drink or something and the last was asking if he was being too pushy? Pushy, no, she thought, keen yes, but she was so glad he was keen. She thought how to respond to the texts.

In the end, she settled on "my place 8pm," and went on to give her address in the Covingham area in Swindon. After the text was gone, she wondered if that was the right thing to do, but decided that the feeling of excitement, she felt deep inside her gut, told her it was the right thing to do, but how to play it, she thought. She didn't want to come over easy, but if she was honest with herself, if she didn't end up in bed with him, she would be disappointed. But she still didn't want to seem that way; but also, she really fancied the pants off him.

"You look like the cat that drank the cream," one of the other nurses said, as Carol walked back into the A&E department. Carol just smiled and flicked her hair and went back to work.

Ben stopped off in a garage on the way to Carols place; he brought a cheap bunch of flowers and a couple bottles of cheap white wine.

When he arrived outside of Carol's house, Ben took a good look around the street, noticing the expensive cars parked on the gravel driveways of the neatly kept gardens, no graffiti of tags or names of people who have had sex with other names written, like there was in the Pinehurst area where he was living.

Ben checked out his reflection in the front door glass, before ringing the bell, he thought to himself "not too shabby," even if I do say so myself.

OMG he is here, Carol thought to herself, as she heard the doorbell chime. On the way to the door, Carol stopped off at her full-length mirror, patted her hair, checked her makeup and finally lifted her breasts up to show off a bit more cleavage. Opening her front door, she treated Ben to a very big and bright smile,

"You found it ok then?" "Yes, no problem at all, I know all the streets in Swindon he boasted."

"Well I'm really glad that you found your way here," she said beaming a big smile, Ben gave Carol the flowers and wine, "Oh Ben, thank you, they are beautiful," and kissed him on the cheek.

"Come on in," she said and led the way in. Ben was admiring her backside as he followed her down the hallway and into the kitchen. Would you like a tea or coffee or something stronger? "When you say something stronger what have you got?" Jill pointed to a shelf in the corner of the kitchen and said, "help yourself; there is vodka, whiskey gin, Baileys, Jack Daniels or the wine you brought." Ben decided on a Jack Daniels and Coke. "What can I get for you?" He asked. "Can I have a large Baileys; you will find ice in the fridge behind you." He passed Carol her drink, "many thanks." By the way would you like something to eat," she asked. "It's a bit of a cheek getting you to cook on our first date," Ben laughed. "No really, I don't mind, I love cooking; I could very quickly rustle up some seabass and salad." "That sounds absolutely delicious, is there anything I can do to help?"

" No, I think I've got it covered, you can just keep the drinks topped up, and keep me amused."

Two hours later, they were sat on the sofa drinking the wine, after a wonderful meal, Carol was feeling totally relaxed in his company, Ben was a little bit fidgety, "what's the matter?" She asked, "I know you're a nurse and I think you think smoking is the worst thing on this planet, but I am really dying for a cigarette, would you mind if I went in your back garden and had a quick one?" "No not at all." Ben went out into the garden and lit his cigarette and had a nose around the garden while smoking his cigarette. Ben was wondering how he could turn the conversation, around to the subject of drugs. As he continued to smoke his cigarette, he hatched a plan.

After he finished his smoke, he went back inside and went to sit on the sofa, making a big show of being in extreme pain by grabbing at his ribs and moaning. Immediately Carol was by his side, putting her arms around him, "aww poor you, you look like you are in so much pain, can I do anything for you?" Ben held Carol tightly and said "I have tried every sort of pain killer you can buy at the pharmacy and nothing is working, then on top of that I'm not registered at any doctors, so I can't go there for a stronger pain relief, the agony is getting unbearable! Someone told me cannabis would help and they gave me this, pulling out a joint from his shirt pocket, but to be honest I'm too frighten to try it, because I don't know how it will affect me." Carol broke away from the embrace they were in; she cupped his face in her hands and kissed him fully on the lips. When she pulled back, she looked into his eyes, "I as a medical professional I'm totally against street drugs, but I have heard that cannabis does help with chronic pain. In a little while why don't you go outside and try it, I will be here to help you if you do have a bad reaction."

Carol put a DVD on and they cuddled down on the sofa. Halfway through the film, Ben said "I think I will go and try this cannabis thingy, if you don't mind."

Ben went outside grinning like a Cheshire cat, right then time to put the second part of my plan into operation.

He lit the joint and made himself cough, trying to make it as bad as possible. He then called out to Carol saying he was feeling lightheaded and dizzy; Carol came outside, put her arm around him, guided him indoors and helped him sit on the sofa, as she lowered him down Ben made a big thing of crying out in pain.

"Well that's not going to work is it!" Carol said. "Let me go upstairs to my medicine cabinet and see what I have got there. Ben was finding it very hard to hide his smile.

When carol back down stairs, she was carrying a box of Co-Codamol tablets. "I have these, which is stronger than the paracetamol you have been taking." "Carol you are a real diamond; you know that don't you." "How about you stop over, then I can keep an eye on you" Carol asked. "Only if you're sure" replied Ben.

5

The next morning, as they sat down for breakfast, Carol asked Ben how he was feeling, "I feel fantastic except for the pain in my ribs." "You didn't seem to be in too much pain whilst we were making love last night." "That is because you are an Angel with a delicate touch, and whilst I was making love to you, pain was the last thing on my mind. It is like you are a natural pain relief, and to help me in my pain I think we ought to do it more often." Ben laughed. "You cheeky sod," she said cheekily, smacking him on the arm. Just then Carols little boy, walked into the kitchen, "Good morning Josh, this is mummies friend Ben," while pointing at Ben. Josh just stared at Ben, then backed up to his mum's legs and hid behind them. "I'm afraid I'm going to have to kick you out now, because I have to get Josh ready for school and then I have to drop him off at my mum's then get to work." "Do you really have to go?" Ben whimpered. "When can I see you again?" He asked. "Oh, let me just check my diary," she pretended to read an imaginary book and said, "As you can see by my diary I am really packed solid at the moment, but I am sure I can fit you in somewhere." She giggled at the double meaning.

Ben made the same movement with his hands, "Yes I'm busy too, but, I will cancel everything, for another date with you." "I am on an early shift today, but then I am going to be on nights for two weeks and Josh will be staying at my mum's, so if you want, we can meet up tonight, but after that it will be a couple of weeks before see each other again."

"I can always come and see you during the day, when you're on night shift." "I will be in bed during the day!" Ben laughed, "that's okay I will come and lay down beside you to keep you warm." Once again, she playfully slapped his arm, and said "what am I going to do with you?" "I can think of a thing or two." "Go on get out of here, I don't want to be late for work, you can text me any time during the day, but it will be impossible to answer a call, also bear in mind that I may not be able to answer your text straightaway please don't think I'm just ignoring you, it's because we are busy." Ben asked Carol how she was going to get to work and she replied by bus.

Ben then asked Carol if she wanted a lift to work as he will be going that way. "That's really nice of you but have to get Josh to my mums first," "That's no problem at all" Ben said. "It will certainly be better than catching and noisy draughty bus." Carol said.

Once everyone was washed, dressed, feed and watered Ben drove Carol to her mums then over to the hospital. Parking up in the ambulance bays, Carol said, "You are not allowed to park here!" "I will only be here a second, I can't have my lady having to walk all through the hospital, were those hunky doctors, might make a pass at you, Carol reached over and kissed Ben; "You have nothing to worry about where that's concerned, I don't want you getting jealous.

She got out of the car and made her way into the hospital, as she went through the glass double doors, she looked back; she waved as Ben pulled away and he returned the wave.

Carol made her way to the changing rooms, as she changed Alice another one of the A&E nurses, came in and said, "Carol whose face was you snogging off outside?" Carol's face went red, and she said, "That's my new boyfriend, his name is Ben." "Where did you meet lover boy? "Alice asked "I met him here, he was admitted the other day, as soon as I saw him, I knew he was something special,

I have never given my number to any patient before, but I just knew he was the one." "Well I will wish you well on your romance, it is about time you had a man in your life apart from your little man. By the way, how is he?" "Josh is really good, loving school, he met Ben this morning." "This! Morning!? Does that mean he stayed over?" "He might have" Carol said, while going redder then a beetroot. "You dirty little madam," Alice laughed.

Ben returned to his dingy flat, he went through his pockets and pulled out a box of tablets he had stolen from Carols medicine cabinet in her bathroom when he got up to go to the loo during the night. "I will get a few quid for these, well Carol that's a little more you have earnt for me" he said to himself.

After showering and getting changed and smoking a joint, Ben made his way to his on / off lover's house. He let himself in through the back door and found Tina slumped in an armchair, clearly high on something. "Tina, wake up you lazy bitch."

Tina tried to stir, but the effect of whatever drug she had taken; prevented her from coming too properly.

Ben grabbed her by the hair and dragged her into the kitchen, where he got hold of a saucepan, filled it with cold water and throw it over Tina. Tina screamed, "Get up you fucking whore," shouted Ben, "I want something to eat right now" He grabbed hold of her and pulled her to her feet. "Now get me something to eat," Tina was shaking and crying while trying to cook some bacon and eggs.

"Will you shut the fuck up!" Ben scream at her, this just made Tina shake and cry even more, Ben stormed back into the kitchen and slapped Tina across the face with such force it sent Tina flying across the kitchen table and her head slamming into the door frame knocking her unconscious. Ben had to move Tina out of the way of the back door; before he left he shouted out a load of obscenities at her and kicked her in the stomach before storming out of the house.

Ben walked to his car like nothing had happened; he got in his car and composed a text for Carol, saying how wonderful she was.

How he had such a great time with her and couldn't wait to see her again and how much of a lucky man he was. Also how gorgeous her little boy was. At the end of the text he had to put in how much he was hurting and that he had been to a pharmacy and was unable to get anything stronger then weak Co-Codamol and that was doing nothing for the pain, could she recommend anything else he could take, or could she get anything for him. He then just drove away from Tina's without a care in the world.

6

As Carol and Alice came out of the changing rooms, they were met by Jason James the new charge nurse who took over the A&E dep't today.

"Morning my lovelies, how are you both on this wonderful day," "Sod off," Alice said jokingly, "We are not used to bright and cheerful this early in the morning, I need at least 5 cups of coffee, before my brain even thinks of waking up." "Come on ladies, it's time for the handover." They all made their way to the A&E office, were the off coming team tell the oncoming team, what had happened during the last shift, what patients are still in the unit and how far along their treatment was. Jason James then gave each nurse their duties, i.e. Resus Children, Adults, Chest Pain and Minor Injuries. Jason James brought the meeting to a close, by telling all the staff both trained nurses and healthcare assistant's, "I believe in each member of staff, is as important as the next, I will not have a department of them and us, we are a team, it's the only way this department can run efficiency and be able to meet the government targets. if you are not busy then find someone who is, and lend a hand, and that way, patient care will always be covered whether they come in very sick or with a splinter, each one will be treated with care, empathy and dignity. Right let's go and meet our adoring patients." With that the meeting broke up and Carol grabbed hold of Alice and said, "What do you think of Jason James?" "Well let's hope he can turn this unit around and get it back to unit where I wanted to come to work and not dreading it." Alice replied.

The smoke alarm at Tina's house, started sounding as the bacon in the frying pan caught fire; very quickly the whole kitchen was engulfed in a black acrid smoke. The flames started licking at the ceiling. Tina's next-door neighbour opened Tina's back door and whoosh the flames shot out of the open door.

Tina was still laid unconscious on the floor Panicking the friend called 999 and asked for all three emergency services, telling the operator she thought that her friend was still inside. No matter how she tried to rouse her, by shouting, there was no sign of Tina. The police were the first to arrive, but they were beaten back by the smoke and flames. Tina's neighbour was screaming for Tina, and it took both police officers to stop the neighbour going into the burning house.

It seemed an eternity before the fire brigade arrived, but the sound of the sirens seemed to help calm the neighbour down. On arrival the fire brigade, got their breathing equipment out and the fireman were in the house and bringing an unconscious Tina out within minutes. The fireman handed Tina over to the paramedics, who had just arrived, they put an oxygen mask on her, but her breathing was very shallow, and her eyes just rolled back in her head. Examining Tina, one of the paramedics noticed Tina's stomach. "I think she is pregnant" he said to the other paramedic.

"We need to roll with this one, get the police to escort us while I contact Swindon Hospital." The paramedic pressed and held the number 1 button on his handset, and across the other side of Swindon the red phone at Swindon Hospital Resus room started to ring.

Swindon Resus" Alice said as she picked up the red phone, "Hi, we are bringing one into you under escort, Female mid to late 20's pulled from house fire, GCS (Glasgow Coma scale) 4, breathing shallow and laboured, soot around nostrils, bruising to face and body, possibly pregnant. Be with you in ten (one zero) minutes."

After putting the phone back into the cradle, Alice picked up the microphone and announced, "Adult and Paediatric call ten minutes."

Under police escort the ambulance was making good time across Swindon, when the paramedic looking after Tina in the back of the ambulance, suddenly shouted for the vehicle to stop. "She is crashing!" The driver brought the ambulance to a sudden stop; it stopped so fast the police car following them, nearly crashed into the back of them.

There was a tap on the back door of the ambulance, the door opened, and a police officer asked, "if all was ok?" One of the paramedics turned around and said, "No her heart has stopped; we are working to get it going again." Ten minutes later they had got a heartbeat very weak but there. Once again, the paramedic contacted Swindon hospital to update them, so as they could have someone from cardiology waiting, when they arrived.

Carol, Alice and Jason James along with various specialists were standing by when the trolley was rushed into Resus, "Quiet Please" said the lead doctor, let's have a clear and precise handover." The bay went quiet, for a second, all you could hear was the bleeping of the monitor showing Tina's heart rate. One of the paramedics cleared his throat and said out loud in a clear voice,

"This is Tina surname unknown, age unknown thought to be in her mid-20's, possibly pregnant. Tina was evacuated from a house fire, by the fire brigade. On first examination her GCS was 4, her "Sats" was 88%, her BP was 75/55, "Resps" 6, Pupils fixed and dilated, soot blacking around nostrils, no foetal heart rate detected. We had a cardiac episode on the roadside; we shocked her 3 times and continued CPR until we got here." "Thank you" said the consultant. He then started giving out orders to continue CPR and check pulses to check blood gases and to run fluids. He ordered an ultra-scan, to check the condition of the baby.

"Stop CPR, any output?" No outputs, chest not rising, no reaction to stimulus, no eye movement, no life signs from mother or baby called out each specialist in turn. The consultant then looked at everyone in the room, "Does anyone want to try one more time or do we call it?"

As the consultant looked around each member of staff, each shook their head as he made eye contact with them. Time of deaths 10.25am.

"Thank you everybody for your efforts, but I think we were on a hiding to nothing on this one. Such a shame we couldn't do more for either one of them. Are there any relatives I need to talk too?"

Without a word the nursing staff went about preparing the young lady for the morgue. Within 15 minutes you wouldn't know what had happened in the Resus room and how 2 people had lost their lives, one never even made it to birth.

7

Sergeant Timms of Swindon Police had the enviable task of informing Tina's parents of what had happened. Sergeant Timms had had dealings with this family before; Tina and her brother Stuart were both well known in the drugs world and to the Police. They both had criminal records an arm's length long, for Drugs, shoplifting and petty crimes. "How I hate this part of the job," he said to the WPC, who had also drawn the short straw back at the station, "even with a family as well-known as this.", as they arrived outside Tina's parent's home. They walked up the garden path just as the rain started pouring down heavily. He braced himself as he knocked on the front door. Tina's father answered the door. Sergeant Timms and the WPC showed their id. "Who is it this time, Tina? Stuart? What have they done?" "Mr Williamson, can we come in please?" said Sergeant Timms.

The Williamson family could best be described as the neighbours you wouldn't want to live next door too, the original neighbours from hell. The father was dressed in grubby stained tracksuit bottoms,

a dirty vest with more holes in it then fabric, unshaven for at least a week, and hair that hadn't seen a comb in ages. He had nothing on his feet; his toenails were blacker then a black snooker ball. The inside of the house was in-between a hovel and slum, all the furniture was dirty, and the floor was barely visible through all the muck and animal faeces.

"Willy is the missus around?" Sergeant Timms asked. "She not up yet, she is still in her pit."

"Willy this is really important, can you go and get her," The tone of Sergeant Timms started to worry Willy, "why what's going on Sergeant?" "Please Willy go get Joan" Instead of going upstairs to get her, he went as far as the bottom of the stairs. Willy shouted at the top of his voice "Joan get your fat arse down here, the law's here and they want to talk to both of us!"

Two thumps on the floor signalled that Joan was out of bed, "what the fuck do they want now; none of the kids live here anymore," Joan shouted down. "Just get down here now. "Willy shouted back up. "For fuck sake, someone better have had died."

Sergeant Timms looked across at the WPC and made a facial gesture, which Willy caught. "Sergeant this is serious isn't!" "I'm not going to lie Willy it is." Just then Mrs Williamson came through the door, dressed in a leopard skin print nightie, which had food stains down the front of it and a pair of UGG boots, which looked like they had been rescued from a rubbish tip. "Well what the fuck do you two want then?" Joan asked bitterly. "I think you better sit down the pair of you."

There was a lot of quizzical looks between the husband and wife.

"I don't know how to say to you, but I have some dreadful news and there is no easy way of saying it. It's your Tina." "What about Tina," Joan interrupted? "I'm getting there, just listen, there was a fire at Tina's house and I'm sorry to tell you she passed away on the way to the Hospital in the ambulance." "NO" screamed Mrs Williamson "NO, NO, NO. "She wailed "Not my little angel," she seemed to stop for a second. "OMG, what about the baby?"

"I'm really sorry the baby didn't make it either. Mrs Williamson threw herself to the floor and was screaming at the top of her voice "My baby! My baby! My baby."

The WPC put her arm around Mrs Williamson, "I am so, so sorry for your loss, I know we have never batted for the same team, but I promise you, we will be here for you all during this tough time."

"Can we go and see her?" "Of course, you can, we will contact the hospital for you and make the arrangements and take you both there." "Oh shit, Stuart, we have to tell Stuart, Willy, phone him now and tell him to come home NOW and not worry about the police car parked outside, come on and do it now for fucks sake."

Stuart arrived home in about 10 minutes; he came bowling through the door shouting, "What the fucks going on? What the fuck are 'THEY' doing here? Pointing at the police officers "Sit down son, we have had some tragic news, Tina's house caught fire, and Tina didn't make it out" Stuart jumped up and started shouting.

"What the fuck do you mean 'FIRE' and Tina didn't make it, how did the fire start." He screamed at Sergeant Timms, "Was the house torched? If it was torched someone is going to die, very painfully." "Now Stuart, don't start making threats like that, as it happens, I have just learnt from the fire brigade, as you were on you way here, that the fire started in the kitchen, in the cooker. Tina must have been cooking something and fell asleep or something like that," he didn't want to tell the family that his own thoughts were that Tina was off her head on something or other. "Have you told Ben mum?" "No. I wanted to tell you first." "I will call him now." Stuart said. He got his phone out and dialled Ben's number.

Ben was just walking into the pub as his phone rang, he saw it was Stuart calling, after giving Tina a slap earlier, he couldn't be bothered with an argument with that pint size prick, so he shoved his phone back into his pocket and ignored it, fuck 'em he thought to himself.

Throughout the afternoon, Ben had stayed in the pub, as the rain outside wouldn't let up and he didn't fancy getting soaked.

His phone had kept ringing all afternoon, every time he looked to see who was calling; it was either Tina's brother or Tina's dad. Maybe I did slap her a bit hard he thought to himself, but the bitch deserved it.

By 5pm, Ben was still at the pub and was well plastered when Stuart walked into the pub, "Why the fuck haven't you been answering your phone? Stuart shouted at him angrily, "We have been trying to get fucking hold of you all fucking day!" "Tina is fucking dead." Ben just stared at Stuart. "Did you hear me; Tina is fucking dead." Ben went as white as a ghost and in a drunken mumble said "What do you mean dead? How is she dead? What the fuck happened?" All the time thinking through a drunken haze, did I kill her when I slapped her? What about when I kicked her, no he thought, it's going to be something else; it's nothing I have done, nothing to do with me,

I didn't kill her. If they thought it was me, Stuart would have come at me with a weapon. No, he thought to himself again, it's nothing to do with me.

8

Carol was just coming to the end of her shift, when her phone buzzed in her tunic top. She saw it was Ben calling her; she waited until it went to answerphone. Then she quickly wrote out a text saying, "busy call you in 20 minutes" and ended the text with 3 kisses, then sent it to Ben.

Ben was still at the pub with Stuart. But this time, he was drinking black coffee, trying hard to sober up fast. "Who were you trying to call?" Stuart asked, "Just a bloke that I was supposed to be meeting later to get some gear off." "You got anything to smoke now?"

Stuart asked Ben. "Yeah let's go and have a smoke." The pair of them went outside and sat down at a table with rain-soaked seats and soaking wet umbrella.

Ben quickly and skilfully rolled a spliff, lit it, took a big drag and passed it over to Stuart. They passed it forward and backward until it was finished, not worrying about the smell or the people walking past.

"What the hell am I supposed to do? Ben asked Stuart, "Do I go up to the hospital, do I go to your mum's place or do I go home,

I really am at a loss of what to do," Ben then put his head into his hands thanking god it was raining so he could pretend to cry. Using the rain to cover up the fact he had no tears. "Come on mate." Stuart said putting his arm around him; you know you will always be a part of our family." "Stu, bud, would you mind if I went home, I need some time by myself to come to terms with what has happened?"

"No probs, mate, if you need me or anything just bell me ok."

Ben was walking towards the taxi rank, because he didn't want to run the risk of driving his car and being stopped by the law,

with what had happened to Tina and him being well known to the police, he didn't want PC Plod putting two and two together and connecting him and Tina's death. When his phone rang, he looked at the screen, seeing it was Carol made him smile. He pressed the answer button, "Hi Carol." "Hi Ben, you called!" "Yeah, I just fancied a chat, but since then I have had some really crappy news and I really could do with having someone to talk to about it. I was wondering if you wanted to meet up."

"I am just about to make my way home, if you want to give me about a couple of hours I want to pop to my mums to see Josh before he goes to bed, then I need to go to the supermarket, then home. Come on over at 7pm and I will do us some dinner, if you want something to eat." "Ok babe see you at 7." "I am looking forward to it," Carol said, "Me too," Ben said and blew a kiss down the phone and Carol blew one back.

After hanging up from Carol, his phone rang again, he thought that it might have been Carol again, but it was one of his customers.

"Dude, what can I do for you?" "Have you got any weed?" "Yeah, how much you want?" "A ten bag," "No probs meet me at mine, I will be back in about 20 minutes, but won't have time for a smoke, as I have to be somewhere else later." "Cheers Ben, see you at yours." "Later, dude."

Ben didn't know if it was the drink, the news about Tina or the fact he was soaked through because of the bloody rain, but he was feeling pissed off, and having to wait hours before seeing Carol was just making it worse.

He finally made it to his flat, taped onto the front door was a letter from his landlord, he went inside, ripped open the letter and what he read just made his mood even blacker. The letter told him because he hadn't paid his rent yet again, he was now being served a 2 months' notice to quit the flat. Fuck the landlord, he'll get some rent when I feel like paying it, not when he demands it, the flat should be condemned anyway, he has a fucking cheek trying to con money out of me for this hellhole, he ought to pay me for living here, he thought.

Ben's mate turned up half an hour later. They did the deal for the cannabis and his mate was gone. He then had a long shower, used half a tin of body spray, brushed his teeth and put on his cleanest clothes, slicked his hair back with gel, looked at himself in the mirror and decided he will try to convince Carol to let him move him with her.

Later that evening, Ben was at Carol's house, sat at the kitchen table with a can of beer in his hand. Carol was sat opposite him with a glass of white wine. "What was the bad news you got today?" she asked. Ben didn't want to let Carol know that he was in a relationship with Tina and that he had been with her today, so he decided to tell her that he had heard that a very close school friend had died in a house fire. "What was her name?" Carol asked, "Tina Williamson" Ben informed her. "OMG" said Carol

"I was on the team that tried to save her in Resus." "You were!" "Yeah, she was worked on by the roadside by the paramedic, and we carried on with CPR trying to save her and the baby." "BABY" Ben said loudly, so much so it took Carol by complete surprised and she wondered if she had said the wrong thing. "Yes, she was pregnant, did you not know?" Ben was away in a world of his own, trying to think how the hell he had forgotten she was pregnant. Tina had only told him a fortnight ago, he hadn't seen her in quite a while, as she was beginning to become very needy and a pain in the arse, saying things like, Ben when are we going to get a place of our own and become a proper couple, you know settle down together and maybe even get married and have children, you know how much I love you and I know you love me. Sod that he had thought to himself, there is no way I'm spending the rest of my life with you. So, he had tried to avoid her, getting one of his minions to drop off her gear and collect the money for it.

Coming back to the real world, once again he had decided to lie, "No I didn't know,

that comes as quite a shock to me as Tina usually tells me everything that was going on in her life." "Oh Ben, I'm so, so sorry, me and my big mouth, please forgive me, you really are having a shit time of it at the moment. How can I make it up to you?" Ben smiled at her and said if I wasn't in so much pain, I could think of a way or two." He said in a laughing manner. "You still have trouble with your ribs?" "Oh, like you wouldn't believe, every movement is extreme agony, so much so that I think the doctors have missed something or haven't told me everything and not having anything stronger then over the counter medication, which by the way is doing absolutely jack shit for my pain. I hate to ask but I don't suppose you have anything stronger or can get me anything stronger from work. I'm still not registered at a GP's, even if I was, I wouldn't be able to get an appointment for weeks and they don't seem to care if they leave you in agony.

All the quacks seem to care is about money, golf and telling people to stop smoking or go on a diet" Carol laughed, "I think they do a little bit more than that, but I can see how some people can see it that way."

"I have some codeine sulphate tablets somewhere, they are stronger then over the counter pills, I will see if I can find them, the last time I saw them they were in the bedroom." "Do you want me to help search the bedroom?" Ben said jokingly. And do you think we would look for the tablets, if we both went up there? Carol giggled. A few minutes Carol came back into the Kitchen and gave Ben a nearly full box of codeine, "Try these, and see if they help you."

For the next few hours Ben and Carol had Dinner a few more drinks then they went upstairs where they made love for what seemed ages, Carol thought to herself, wow this guy is incredible. She had never felt like this before, and as for doing the other things she thought she would have completely refused before, she found herself more than willing and to her amazement she actually enjoyed it.

As for Ben, he knew he had her completely were he wanted her, not much longer then he would start to push her to get what he wanted, 'CONTROLLED' drugs

9

After spending the night together, Carol and Ben had a leisurely morning, having breakfast then making love again. Then showering together.

Carol said that she needed to go and see her son, as she was now on nights for two weeks and wouldn't get to see him much.

So early in the afternoon Ben went off home and Carol went round to her mums to see Josh.

As Ben turned into his street, he saw a police car parked outside of his flat. He quickly braked, put the car into reverse and drove away panicking, why are they looking for me?

Meanwhile Carol arrived at work later that evening, her mood was so good, even the cold grey sky and the constant drizzle couldn't dampen her spirit. Coming out of the changing room, she bumped into Jason,

"Evening your highness," Carol quipped, "less of the cheek, more of doing the nursing thing," Jason replied.

"I've just popped my head into the waiting room, looks like the usual mixture of sore fingers and I need a sick note because I didn't feel like going to work for a week or two, I know there is nothing wrong with me, but I am going to try and convince you otherwise. But you don't have to worry about them, I've put you, Lizzie and Alice in Resus, I'm going to be floating between Resus and Minors but if we get a red phone I will be straight in. If you can get the keys off sister before she goes off duty and keep them on you, you are responsible for the drugs cabinet tonight." Jason continued. "But what happened to the rule that only a sister grade was allowed to be the keyholder." Carol asked. "It's one of the changes I have come up with some others, I have got management to agree to. To try and improve efficiency in the dept.

Carol found the Sister in charge and asked for the keys, "Have you done a drugs level check?" Carol asked, "I haven't had time to wipe my nose let alone do a level check!" Sister said. "Would you like me to do it now? Carol asked, "If you wouldn't mind, then bring me the paperwork and I will sign it off, before I get to go home."

Carol went to the cabinet and started to check how many of each drug they had in the cabinet, when it came to the stronger medication, Carol found herself thinking about Ben and the pain he was in. They wouldn't miss one box, she thought to herself, after all the cabinet is in constant use and somebody could have forgotten to fill in the log book properly. When it came a very strong pain killer called co-dydramol or DF118 as they are more commonly known, Carol marked down 1 box less then there actually was, she could easily say she had miscounted them if anyone was to challenge her before she got Sister to sign off on the drugs log.

The next hour or so of Carol's shift went by without a single patient. The Resus staff was enjoying a cup of coffee, when a trainee nurse came into the department sat down with a coffee, "It's very quiet tonight." As one, the staff all said, "don't say the Q word, but it was too late, the red phone started ringing, "What did I say wrong?" asked the trainee nurse, "You never use the word 'quiet' in this department, because if you use it, the red phone is bound to ring, with an emergency call to shatter the peace, just like it did just now."

"Swindon Resus" Carol said as she picked the red phone. Grabbing a form from under the desk she wrote, 73-year-old female, with a suspected left sided stroke 15 minutes out. Just as Carol replaced the phone into its receiver and went to pick up the microphone the phone started to ring again. Turning to the trainee nurse, she said, "See what I mean, get ready to be run off your feet, and yes we will blame you, she laughed." The trainee nurse apologised and promised never to use that word again in this department. Carol picked up the red phone again and the voice on the other end said, "Cyclist versus car, male late teens, bulls eyed the windscreen, open fracture left tib and fib, deep laceration to forehead, possible fractures of left side ribs and possible bleeding into the pelvis, GCS 8 on arrival, now 12 wrapped and packed arrival 20 minutes."

Carol put down the phone picked up the microphone and announced, "Stroke team to Resus, 15 minutes." She then continued "Major trauma team to Resus 20 minutes."

Jason came running into Resus, "What the hell is happening out there tonight?" he asked Carol. "Someone used the 'Q' word, that's what happened." "Okay what patient is going into which bay" he asked, "trauma into 1 and stroke into 3, both teams called and on way," "Right, the trauma straight to CAT scan on arrival we will assess there, I'll take that, I want you to take the lead nurse role for the stroke victim and run with her, any problems shout out, but I have every confidence you can handle this one by yourself as lead. It's really important as lead you listen to everything that is being said, even while you are busy with the patient, if you hear that a clot busting drug Alteplase can be given, write down the time you heard it and when it was given and who authorised it. After the problems they had at Nottingham, when the drug was given twice, and the patient bled out and died, and both the consultant and his registrar denied hearing the other one calling for the drug to be given, or seeing the drug actually being administered. We will not have that happening here okay? So, remember ears open the whole time."

Carol was both scared and excited, as this was her first ever lead and she didn't want to mess up in any way, so she double checked everything, she thought Alice might take umbrage at her friend telling her what to do, but from the time the patient arrived to the time she was taken to the stroke ward everything ran as smooth as silk, which can be more then said with what was happening with Jason's patient.

Jason met the ambulance crew by the main doors, "straight to CT and we will do a handover while the patient is being prepped for the scanner." They arrived at the scanner just as the patient's heart stopped, "Back to Resus" one of the doctors shouted, and everyone turned and ran back to the Resus room. They worked on the patient for about 10 minutes until he was stable enough to go back to be scanned. Once again as they were scanning him this time his blood pressure hit the deck. Picking up the phone, Jason called the Theatre suite, "we may be bringing one up to you in a few minutes can you prepare for internal bleeding into the pelvis, I will let you know more as soon as the boss has had a chance to make her decision." The radiographer stopped the scan and the consultant, and her team rushed into the Scanning room and began a head to toe examination. "Jason" "Yes Dr Michaels," "Good call on alerting theatres, can you call them and tell them we are on our way and it is a bleed in the pelvis, also call the blood bank and get 6 units of 'O' neg down to theatres and be ready for more if needed, as I don't want to be hanging around for them to cross match in the first place, they can cross match once we get the 'O' neg running." "Will do and I will bleep the ortho team on call, to join you in theatre, is there anyone else you want bleeping?" "No that will do for the minute, let's just get rolling!"

Five hours later, the patient was in Intensive care recovering from having the bleeding stopped in his pelvis, his leg being put into a temporary cast when his blood pressure crashed again, he was rushed back into theatre where they found the source of the bleeding, this time it was his spleen, which they removed just in time to save his life.

While Jason was busy with his patient and the rest of Carol's team were busy cleaning up, she went to the drugs cabinet and removed the co-dydramol and went into the staff room and put the drugs into her handbag, all the time worrying if she was doing the right thing, but it was too late now to go back. Ben will be so grateful when I give him these, she thought to herself. She knew it was wrong and that this was the first time she had stolen anything in her life, but her Ben was in pain and she could help him get out of pain, so in her mind that justified her taking the pills.

Carol decided she wanted to see Ben after work, so she sent him a text asking if he wanted to pick her up at 8am from work. He quickly responded he would be no problem to pick her up. That text made Carol feel like everything was perfect and how happy she was.

10

Ben had driven around for hours, all through the night his mind was turning faster than it had ever turned before, He'd parked up in one area of Swindon, he would then spot a passing patrol car and he would drive away before being spotted, he was so sure that every Police officer was out looking for him. He went from area to area not having a clue what to do. His phone kept ringing, but he didn't answer it as he had heard that the Police could track his phone if he answered it.

By 6am, Ben was parked up in a local beauty spot, his eyes were heavy, he was feeling hungry but more than that he had ran out of weed, he was just considering about going to a 24-hour burger drive thru, when he had received the text from Carol, asking if he wanted to pick her up from work. He looked at his watch, it was just after 6, and Carol didn't finish until 8, so he had a couple of hours to kill.

Ben thought about who might be up and about this early in the morning and would have some weed he could smoke.

Looking through his list of contacts, he came across Rob, Rob was a night owl and he always had a stash. He made his way to Rob's flat and knocked on the door. "Ben what are you doing up this early in the morning?" "I have a lot on my mind and just couldn't sleep, so I thought I would go out for a drive," he lied. "I'm really sorry to hear about Tina, no wonder you can't sleep. How are you holding up?" "In pieces," he lied again, "She was my world, my soulmate, and I'm so lost without her." He continued to lie, really piling on the hurt he was supposed to be feeling. "Do you want a smoke?" "Yeah why not," Ben replied, "I have to be at the hospital at 8, something to do with identifying Tina." He lied again, not wanting Rob to know that he was picking up his latest conquest. "I thought Tina's family would have done the ID," Rob said, "They were supposed to, but when it came to it, they were so upset that they just couldn't go through with it, so they asked me to do it instead, and of course I agreed, it's the least I could do." The lies rolled off Bens tongue as easily as a marble rolling across the floor.

There was a very heavy scent of Cannabis inside the flat, and a faint whirl of a cooling fan, "You are growing your own now?" Ben asked.

"I have been for a little while now," Rob said, "this will be my third harvest, I don't sell it, and it is all for my personal use and of course anyone I want to share a spliff or two with." He laughed. "Talking of which, you have a tug or two on this one, fancy a drink"

Ben gladly accepted the spliff, taking a big drag on it, holding the smoke in his mouth for a short while, trying to get the most effect out of it, slowly he exhaled, and said "this is some good stuff Rob, if you ever want to sell any, just let me know and I will have it off you in a heartbeat.

Coffee, milk with 3 sugars." "No probs,"
"So when will you be harvesting your
crop?" Ben asked, "In about a week, then
another week to 10 days to dry, then it will
be ready for smoking." Ben sat there
thinking to himself, if you don't sell it all to
me, I will arrange for a late-night visit from
some big boys and just take what I want and
fuck you for not selling. Rob brought the
drinks in and Ben thanked him by saying
"A friend in need is a friend in deed but a
friend with weed the best." "Cheers" said
Rob as Ben passed the spliff back to Rob.

Ben looked at his watch and saw the time
was fast approaching 7.30, he thanked Rob
for the drink and the smoke said bye and
left.

Carol saw Ben parked by the main entrance
to the hospital, she gave him a big smile
and a wave, Ben waved back and reached
across to open the passenger door. As Carol
got into the car, she leant over to kiss Ben;
she sniffed the air and said, "My god you
stink of cannabis,

what have you been doing?" Once again Ben put his lying brain into top gear and said, "Oh that, I had some time to kill, so I went to see my mate Rob, you know, the one that gave me that wacky baccy to smoke, (not wanting to let on, he knew all the words, slang and proper for cannabis, to try and hide is innocence, well his place reeks of it and he was smoking a wacky cigarette while I was there, so I suppose it must have got onto and into my clothing."

"I think when we get back to my place, you can get right in the shower and I will put your stuff through the washing machine."

Ben made a big thing of leaning across to Carol and sniffing the air, "You stink of the hospital as well, so I think you need to put your uniform in the wash and join me in the shower," Ben laughed.

Carol started to blush and said, "as long as you wash my back, I will agree." "Back! not only do I intend to wash your back I'm going to take great delight in washing your front as well."

73

This made Carol go bright red, "Just start the car and get me home fast," she managed to blurt out. "Oh, by the way I have a surprise for you later." She added. "Let's hope it's something sexual," Ben said, Carol reached over and playfully thumped his arm. "Hey that hurt," Ben said pretending to be in pain, "You'll pay for that later," he said, "Well let's hope it's something sexual" Carol replied with a huge smile on her face.

Within 5 minutes of arriving at Carol's they were both naked and in the shower. "So, what's the surprise then?" Ben asked, "Well first this," she said dropping to her knees, but the other one will have to wait a while.

An hour or so later, they were cuddled up in bed, "That was one hell of a surprise in the shower, I don't think the next one could better that." Carol jumped out of bed and ran naked downstairs, and came back to the bedroom with her handbag, she reached inside and pulled out the box of Co-dydramol,

"I borrowed these from work," she said, throwing the box over to Ben. "What are they?" Knowing full well what they were and how much he could get for each tablet. "They are called Co-dydramol or DF118's, and they are the next step up in the pain killer range." Carol said, getting back into bed. "My god, thank you so much," Ben said and to show my appreciation I have a surprise for you." He threw the bed cover onto the floor and began kissing Carol lower and lower.

11

Ben left Carol's mid-afternoon, saying he wanted to go and see a friend. He was on the phone trying to sell the tablets before he even reached his car. Within 4 phone calls Ben had sold half the tablets. Ben's phone rang; he looked at the caller id and saw it was 30.

30's real name is David Jones. David Jones is a detective sergeant in the Wiltshire Police Drug Squad. The reason he was known to the underworld as 30, was because if he found out you were selling drugs, you had to pay him 30% of the profit or he would have you arrested for suppling the drugs or he would fabricate something else for you to be arrested for. Firstly, to teach you lesson and secondly to show you who was the boss. He liked to be called 30, so that his own name was never used in a call or in a text, and that meant nothing could be led back to him.

Ben touched the button to answer the call, "30" he said, "What can I do for you?"

"A little bird has told me you are offloading some DF118's. How many have you sold and how many have you got left?"

As quick as a flash Ben said, "I have sold 14 and have 14 left to sell," leaving out the fact the Carol had given him 56 tablets, this way he would only have to give him 30% on the 28 and not on the whole lot. "And where did you get 28 DF118's?" 30 asked, Ben had already thought of an answer to this question when he saw who was calling him, "I stole them off my sister's husband, who has hurt his back. The doctor had given him 2 weeks' supply, but he doesn't like taking strong stuff, so as I left, I just picked them up and put them in my pocket, he won't create a fuss when he realizes they are missing. My sister might, but she can go to hell."

"How much are you charging for each tablet? Bearing in mind I already know, I just want to see if you are lying to me!"

Ben was unsure if 30 really did know, but he wasn't going to take that chance. "I'm getting a ten spot for tab," Ben said, "So that makes it 42 quid you owe me, lets round it up to a Bullseye (£50) and a Monkey (£100) once you sold the rest!"

Ben knew if he didn't bitch about being charged so much, 30 will guess he had more then he said. "Come on 30, give me a break,

I'm skint and need every penny I can get my hands on." "Think yourself lucky I'm not taking more, and if I hear you've been bad mouthing me about it; you'll be seeing the inside of a cell faster than you can say stitch up. Meet me at the Circle at 9pm and don't be late!"

Ben spent the rest of the afternoon and evening going here and there selling the tablets and buying weed and cocaine, then selling the Cocaine on for a big profit. He was so busy ducking and diving, he forgot he promised Carol he would pick her up and take her to work. When Carol called him at 7.30pm to find out where he was, he lied saying his car had broken down and for her to get a taxi and he would give her the money in the morning when he would pick her up if she wanted.

Carol had awoken a few hours earlier, wishing Ben had stayed over, but he had made some excuse about going to see a friend and she wondered to herself if it was a female 'friend'.

Carol admonished herself for feeling jealous, she had only just got to know Ben, she told herself and he may well have friends who were female, it doesn't mean they were having sex, just because she had always been cheated on in the past doesn't mean to say Ben is like that, he doesn't seem the kind and not only that he always answered the phone or text back quickly and offered to take her to work or collect from work, if he was in another relationship he wouldn't be able to do those things.

But when Ben didn't show up, to take her to work, her jealous mind started all over again.

By the time Carol got into work, she wasn't in the best of moods. In the changing rooms, Lizzie picked up on Carol's mood, "What's up sweetie, love lost its flavour already?" No not really, Ben was supposed to pick me up, but he said his car had broken down, I have no reason to disbelieve him, but I also wanted him to stay over this afternoon but he said he couldn't, he has promised to pick me up in the morning even if he has to borrow a car plus he said he would pay for my taxi today, so I can't be hard on him yet." "What do you mean yet and as long as he is 'hard' on you I don't know what you are talking or worrying about," giggled Lizzie. Carol put her arms around Lizzie and gave her a big hug, "It's just me being stupid, now let's get moving before we get on the wrong side of Jason and end up mopping up blood and gut's all night."

Carol and Lizzie walked into the staff room for the handover to discover it had been a really busy day and it was showing no signs of slowing down.

"Right then <u>Bay 1</u>," the sister who was going off duty said, "Is a 67 yo female called Gloria, 'MI' now stable waiting to go to the cardiac ward.

<u>Bay 2</u> Female called Helen, early 20's overdose on heroin, again stable, the bed manager is trying to find her a mental health bed, but that's like looking for a half of a needle in a king size haystack. So, expect her to be with you all night unless a miracle happens.

<u>Bay 3</u> Young lad aged 7 called Shaun with an open fracture to his right leg after falling through the gap on his trampoline at home, ortho doc's will be taking him to theatre shortly.

<u>Bay 4</u> Is a male no id, overdosed on god knows what, age unknown approx. 30 upwards, totally unresponsive Doc's are working on him as we speak.

<u>Bay 5</u> is now free and with that my lovelies as the saying goes I'm outta here."

Jason stood up and said "Thank you Julie, Okay, Alice and Carol you have Resus along with myself, I will be the key holder, Jeanette, Sarah, Kevin and Lisa you have Minors, Jeanette you will have lead there, any problems come and find me or bleep me on 4266.

Nursing auxiliaries, Sam and Jo you will be in Resus, Bridget Catherine and Emma you will be in Minors under Jeanette.

Right boys and girls it's time to go and play."

The first part of Carols shift was fairly mundane; it wasn't until just after 11pm when the red phone went off for the first time.

Carol picked up the phone "Swindon Resus." "Good evening" said the voice on the other end of the line, "This is the air ambulance crew, we are bringing you a 25 yo male, who has been bitten by a pet snake, on his left arm, the problem is we don't know what snake has bitten him, but we do know that there are 3 snakes here and all are dangerous and are all here illegally. They have not been de-venomed.

We have arranged for the police to contact someone who knows about snakes and who can identify them and tell us just how poisonous they are. You will need to contact the UK National Poisons Information service and put them on standby. The patient has a GCS of 5, BP 100/68, pulse weak but identifiable, Shortness and difficulties in breathing. We will be with you in 15 minutes by helicopter, can you have the helipad team ready and lights switched on please." Carol said she would get on with it straight away, "Jason" Carol called out, "you better come over here and see this before I announce it." "Oh shit" Jason said, "I've had to deal with this kind of case before, right let me think, call it out as a male trauma, and I will ring the blood bank to see which Haematologist to wake up, can you call the NPU and have them on speaker phone ready for when we know what we are dealing with."

Carol put out the trauma call and then got straight onto the phone with the NPU and spoke with a warm sounding person. After giving her all the details, the lady on the other end said "Are you sure you a dealing with a poisonous snake and not an Adder?" "At the moment" said Carol "we have no idea what we are dealing with; we are awaiting an expert to identify the snake, so we can let you know." If your expert can not identify it tell someone to take a photo and send it to my office, we can identify almost anything here."

When the patient arrived 15 minutes later, he was having extreme breathing difficulties and the onset of paralysis. Minutes later a policeman came running into Resus, "It's an Australian Tiger Snake." Carol Immediately told the person at NPU that it was an Australian Tiger snake. "OK I will send you 5 vials of CSL Tiger Snake Antivenom by helicopter. Can you pass this information onto the doctor dealing with the case, a splint must be used so as the arm does not bend!

The Antivenom will be with you in approx. 30 to 45 minutes keep the patient flat and if possible keep the arm lower than the heart."

The minutes past slowly as the staff waited for the helicopter, everyone was pacing around looking at their watches, wishing it would hurry up and arrive. Carol even went outside to see if she could hear the helicopter. Finally, 25 minutes later the sound of the helicopter's rotor blades could be heard chopping in the cold clear night sky. The Antivenom was rushed into the Resus room and the doctor administered the first vial, just as the monitoring machine alarm sounded and was showing a flat line where it should be showing the bouncing heart rate. The team worked on the patient for another 10 minutes, but the young man was pronounced dead at 12.28 am.

The mood in Resus in fact the whole of the A&E department was sombre and quiet for the rest of the shift.

No one really felt like talking, in a way it was a good job that no more patients came through the doors for the next short while.

Carol sat in the staff room with a cup of coffee, thinking about how she was not really accusing but suspecting Ben of cheating on her, and how silly she had been to even think that, when life can be taken away so quickly but then again so can love, and as she had just found it after a long time. She wasn't going to let her insecurities get in the way of a blooming relationship with her Ben

12

Ben had kept his 9.00 appointment with DS Jones at the Circle, Ben was waiting for him with he arrived, DS Jones pulled up next to Bens car, so that they were parked drivers side to driver's side. DS David Jones was in his mid-30's overweight 5 feet 7 which made his weight problem stand out even more, balding, unshaven, if you saw him, a police officer would be the last thing you would expect him to do as a job. Ben unwound his window as did DS Jones, "Evening Benny boy, you got something for me?" Ben handed over 10 ten-pound notes, "Thank you nicely and don't you forget if I hear your selling and you haven't told me about it you know what will happen right?" "Yeah I do" answered Ben. "By the way that was some shit news about Tina; I had quite a soft spot for our Tina!" Ds Jones said. I know a spot of yours that wasn't so soft, every time you went around there, Ben thought to himself, Tina had told me she had to go down on you every time you went around there, or you would threaten to nick

her for something or other you asshole.
"Yeah it is sad news," said Ben. "I thought
you two had a thing going on" enquired DS
Jones, "Nah we haven't seen each other for
quite a while, the last I heard she had some
other geezer living with her, one of her
junkie mates I no doubt." "Oh right!" said
the DS quizzically. "Anyway, life goes on,
onwards and upwards eh Benny Boy!" Go
fuck yourself, Ben thought to himself, but
said "yeah onwards and upwards." With
that DS Jones pulled away and was gone
with a screech of his tyres. "I hope you rot
in hell dirty 30." Ben shouted out aloud,
and then quickly looked around him to
make sure no one had heard him. Ben then
drove home to get some sleep before
picking Carol up as promised; hopefully she
would have some more stuff for him in the
morning.

Ben had just got into bed, when there was a
loud knock on his door; wearily he
stumbled to door and said, "Who is it?"
"It's me Stuart," came the reply, "Come on
open the door its bloody freezing out here."

Ben opened the door, "What do you want this time of the night?" "Someone said you had some Charlie for sale, have you got any left?" "You could have just called," Ben said annoyed. "But I thought if you had any, I could do a line here?" Well your journey has been wasted as I have sold it all on; all I have got is a bit of weed!" "Shit I really fancied doing a line, have you got any 'E's' or anything to keep me awake?" "Don't you listen?"

Ben said, getting really pissed off now, "All I've got is a bit of weed!" "Who did you sell the Charlie too, maybe they have got some left, can you ring them and find out for me? But first give me your tin and I will roll us a smoke."

Reluctantly Ben passed over his tin containing his weed, tobacco and cigarette papers to Stuart.

Ben went into his bedroom to get his phone and he noticed that he had received a message from Carol, saying she was having a crazy night at work and couldn't wait to see him in the morning.

On his way back through to the living room, Ben stopped off in the kitchen and filled the kettle up and switched it on. "Do you want a drink?" Ben asked. "Have you got any alcohol?" "There may be a little left in the vodka bottle, but I haven't got anything to go with it." "That's ok I will drink it neat anyway.

Ben made himself a cup of coffee putting 5 sugars into it, he went to the fridge to get the milk only to discover what was left in there had gone off, fuck it, I will drink it black.

By the time Ben sat back down in his chair Stuart had rolled the spliff and was in the process of lighting it. He took a big drag on it, inhaled it and almost immediately started coughing. "My god that's some strong skunk you've got there," Stuart said in-between coughs. "I only get the best stuff for myself," said Ben reaching over and taking the spliff off Stuart. After taking a couple of drags he passed it back to Stuart and picked up his coffee, blowing across the top of the cup, trying to cool the coffee down enough to take a sip. "Are you going to make that call?" Stuart asked. "Give me a sec to have a drink then I will do it." Stuart went to pass the spliff back to Ben, who just sat there staring into space. He was thinking about Carol and how to handle her. "Hey Mork calling Orson," Stuart laughed, "You can come back to earth now. What were you thinking about? Stuart asked. "I was thinking about your sister," Ben lied. "It must be hitting you as hard as it's hitting us." Stuart said sympathetically.

"It sure is, I miss her like crazy, I can't even bring myself to go anywhere near her place, it's just too raw." "I know what you mean, we are really cut up, but mum and dad they are just wandering around like zombies." "I really feel for them" Ben lied.

"The autopsy was carried out yesterday, the thought of my sister laid on that cold slab being cut open is just something I can't even start to come to terms with, why they had to cut her open, when it is obvious she died because of the smoke is beyond me." "I know what you mean bro, it's like she is being abused. They just need to leave her alone and let her rest in peace." Ben said.

Ben took a drag on the spliff, passed it back to Stuart, he scrolled through his contact list until he found Kevin's number, he pressed the call button and waited for the call to be answered, "Alright Ben," Kevin said when he answered the phone, "what can I do for you man?" "Have you got any of that coke left?" "Sure have, you want to come over and party?" "No not me, you know Stuart Williamson." "Sure do, it was his sister that died in the house fire wasn't it." "One and the same, well he is looking to party, I'll give him a bag of smoke for you all to share, to make up for the money cos he is broke." "Yeah no probs man, send him over, he will be alright here."

Ben wrote the address down for Stuart. Handing over a bag of weed, "there you go bud, go and party." "Cheers Ben, you're a good mate," You will owe me big time for this you little creep, Ben thought to himself.

After Stuart had left Ben put his phone onto silent, finished his coffee and headed for bed once again. He fell asleep as soon as his head had hit the pillow, and what seemed like 2 minutes later, Bens alarm was going off, reaching out to switch it off, Ben thought to himself, fuck this for a game of soldiers, it's not even light out there, he was so tempted to roll over and go back to sleep and sod Carol, but she may just have some more stuff he could sell, so he made the effort got up showered and put on clean clothes, so he didn't smell of cannabis again. As he walked out of the door, the sun was just peeping through the clouds, promising to be a warm day; well at least it's not pissing down Ben thought as he climbed into his car.

13

Detective Inspector Patrick Jamerson, head of the Swindon serious crime unit, or SCU for short, arrived in his office at 6.30am, the same time as he had done for the past 28 years. To say he was a creature of habit was a complete understatement. Rain snow or sun or even if he had been called out during the night, you would find the DI at his desk, perfectly dressed, in a two-piece dark charcoal grey suit, white shirt, blue tie and highly polished shoes, not a hair was out of place. The DI took great pride in his appearance, his work desk was exactly the same, everything in its place neat and tidy. A cup of black coffee no sugar was sat on its mat on the right side of his desk. A lined A4 pad was placed in the centre of the desk, with his fountain pen, resting on top of the pad. His in and out trays were carefully placed towards the left edge of his desk. In the in tray were all the things that had come in to the office after he had left for the day at 6 o'clock the last evening.

He picked up the first file from the top of pile; he placed his reading glasses on the tip of his nose, just above his perfectly trimmed moustache, which had grown for the Movember charity.

Opening the front cover, it was an autopsy report of a young lady called Tina Williamson, who had died in a house fire. Well the must be some doubt about the cause of death if it has landed on my desk, he thought to himself. He carefully read through the whole document, making sure that he didn't miss a single word.

The DI then fired up his computer, while waiting for the computer to fully load, he reread the report. Once the computer was up and running, he entered Tina's full name date birth and address and waited to see what it churned out. What he read told him Tina had a charge sheet a mile long, and out on police bail for 2 outstanding charges for possession which was waiting for a court date. She had spent 4 months in prison on an 8 months' sentence for possession and supply of a class A drug. Reading the autopsy report, it looked like someone had attacked her and left her unconscious before the fire started and this peeked his interest.

Was the fire started to hide the attack? He asked himself. He went through the file and pulled out the fire brigade report.

Reading through the report, the investigating fire officer had reported that the fire had started in, or around the Cooker area. Whether or not, the fire was set deliberately, is inconclusive, but his best guess was, it was accidental.

By 7.00am the first of his team had started to arrive into work. When the whole team had arrived, the DI left his inner office and walked into the main SCU office. "Good Morning all," He said to those present, first off, has anyone seen the DS this morning? As we have a suspicious death come in overnight, Jenny can you set up an incident room, David and Roly, can you clear the decks of any outstanding cases that can be put on the back burner for a while!"

Just then Detective Sergeant Keith Gregory walked into the office, "Morning campers," he said in a really camp voice, DS Gregory was the complete opposite of his DI, he was always late, and he was never in a suit, just crumpled up chinos and a baggy tee shirt, his hair was too long for the DI's liking and his desk resembled a bomb site.

But the reason the DI let that all go, was that the DS was very good, no, excellent at what he did, his ratio of solved crimes that gained a conviction, was well over 80%. And the fact that he was a 48-year-old gay man; had nothing to do with his fast rise in the DI's department. If all my team could match the DS's success rate, there wouldn't be an unsolved crime in Swindon, the DI thought to himself.

"You have decided to join us then Keith?" "Have I ever let down?" Keith replied. "I don't think it would hurt you to be on time once in a while." The rest of the team took no notice of the conversation between the two, as they had heard it time and time again.

"Right back to the matter in hand, Tina Williamson!" said the DI, "What's our Tina up to now?" The DS asked. "You know or rather you did know of her then?" The DI said. "I had quite a few dealings with the Williamson family when I was in uniform." The DS added. "Well Tina turned up dead in a house fire, the coroner's report states that Tina was knocked unconscious before the fire started, now the FB investigator cannot say for certain that the fire was started deliberately or not, so it's down to us to find out the truth behind this young lady's death. Jenny is going set an incident room, while the rest of the team clear the decks, then this is going to be our main goal.

We need to find out who gave her a smack and when they did it and why they did it. We also need to talk to family, friends, boyfriends or partners. The colour and depth of the bruising indicates she was attacked just a short time before the fire took hold. "Keith do you know anything about Tina's friends, associates or enemies? Did she have a partner or a boyfriend / husband?" The DI asked. "As I said earlier, I had a lot of dealings with the family a few years back, her parents, as far as we know, are not involved in any criminal activities. Their kids, Tina and Stuart, on the other hand, it's all petty crimes like shop lifting, being drunk in public, minor possession of both class A and B. Stuart has a couple of TWOC's driving with no licence or insurance, he has more points on his licence that he actually does not have yet, then Britain have got in the last ten years at the Eurovision Song Contest. Tina was seeing another small-time dealer called Ben Thorton, he was handy with his fist against women, but he would run a mile if he had to go up against a man. Their relationship was very much on and off, so whether he is still on the scene, I have no idea. I will speak to the drug squad to see what they have in relation to Tina or Ben or anyone else who has been on the scene.

DS Jones has had a lot to do with the family, so I will give him a call and pick his brains."

"Okay ladies and gents let's get things moving and solve this case before lunch, just like they do on TV, and if you do solve it before lunch I will not be taking you all out for a meal and drinks." The DI laughed. Boo's rang out around the room.

14

Carol was delighted to see Ben's car parked outside the front entrance as she walked out of the hospital. The sun was already warming the air, without a cloud in the sky, it promised to be a beautiful day. As Carol walked towards Ben's car, even the birds were singing. Ben saw Carol walking towards him with a big smile on her face, hopefully that means she has something for me, Ben thought to himself.

Carol opened the door to the car, "hi honey" she said, "morning sexy," Ben replied, "good shift?" "We had a case which none of us even the doctors have ever had to deal with before." "Oh yeah, what was that then." "A guy got bitten by a poisonous pet snake, we had helicopters flying here there and everywhere, to get the antidote, but in the end, he died. It was quite sad, really."

On the drive to carol's place, Ben turned to carol and said "Did I leave those tablets at yours, as I have looked everywhere for them,

I remember taking 2 tablets at yours, but for the life of me I can't find the rest." Carol thought that's weird, that's the second box of pill's Ben has misled, "Do you often lose things?" Carol asked Ben, "NO" Ben answered sharply, "sorry I didn't mean anything by it," Carol apologised. "No, I'm the one who should be sorry, speaking to you like that, it just I'm in a lot of pain." Ben leant over and gave her a kiss on the lips, "I don't suppose you managed to get anything today, did you?" "I'm really sorry, but it is very difficult to get any tablets or medicines out, unless you are the one responsible for the drugs cabinet keys. The new person in charge of the department, Jason is ultra-sharp with the keys and who has them, if he is in the unit, which is most of the time, he has the keys, so unless he gets called away then no one has access to the cabinet." "What about the ones you have to give to the patients?" "Carol just looked at Ben in disbelief, "Are you honestly saying that I shouldn't give my patients the drugs they desperately need?"

"Well you say you love me and I thought you would want to help me with my pain, which is probably as bad as anyone of them."

The rest of the journey to Carol's house was driven in silence. Ben pulled up outside of the house. He switched off the engine and was about to take his seat belt off when carol said, "look, I am really tired and want to get full days' sleep, so if you don't mind I will go in by myself." Carol then got out of the car. Ben muttered something under his breath, slammed the car into gear and drove off screeching the tyres. Not seeing that as carol entered the house, she was crying.

As carol was showering, she wondered to herself if she had yet made another mistake with her choice of men. She wanted to text Ben and tell him not to pick her up this evening to take her to work. You need to cheer yourself up young lady she told herself. Instead of going to bed to get some much-needed sleep, she rang her mum to make sure that she was going to be in this morning, so she could pop over to see her and Josh, before going to bed.

A shower a quick coffee and carol was out of the door on her way to her mum's.

Thirty minutes' carol was sat in her mum's kitchen with a cup of coffee and best of all she was getting a massive cuddle from her little boy, who was so pleased to see his mum, even though he was used to not seeing mummy for a while when she had to work nights, he understands as much as a 4-year-old could understand.

But right now, none of that mattered as his mummy was here and he didn't want to let her neck go.

Carol's mum looked at her daughter's face and said, "Come on then, tell me what's going on? You look shattered and I can see you are upset about something. Is it to do with work? Or is it the new man in your life? Has he dumped you already?" "No mum! I just had a really hard shift, we had a case in which a young man ended up losing his life, no matter how hard we tried and for some reason it got to me." Carol said only telling the half-truth, leaving out what had happened with Ben. "That's unusual for a death to affect you," "they all affect me, I hate it when we lose a patient, but this one for some reason is different, I suppose it's because it was a case that none of the team had ever dealt with before."

"What was the case, I know you are not supposed to talk about them, but for this to affect you in this way, maybe it would be better to talk about it?" "It's nothing gory or secret, it was a young man got bitten by a snake and died because of it." "Snake bite!" Carols mum exclaimed, "I didn't think we had poisonous snakes in England!"

"We don't, it was an illegally imported snake from Australia." "Oh right." "Anyway, mum as much as I have enjoyed my cuddle with my little man, I need to get home and get some sleep, phone you later to say goodnight to Josh."

Bens temper had calmed down a short while later, you are an idiot, he thought to himself, you could have ruined the best source of legal drugs you ever could have had. You need to put this right and fast.

Ben pulled into a garage picked up a big bunch of flowers, noticing the cashier was busy and not taking any notice of him, he got into his car and drove away without paying for them. He then drove back to carols house put the flowers up against the front door, pushed the bell, got back in his car and drove away.

As carol walked up to her house, she could see there was something by her door. As she got closer she could see it was a bunch of flowers, aww ben must have been back, that's so sweet, it didn't even matter that he had left the price tag on and that he got them from a garage, it's the thought that counted, she thought to herself.

15

DS Gregory had to make a call, he just didn't want to make. He had to call the most bigoted homophobic police officer he ever had the misfortune to have met. Come on then, let's get this over with, he thought to himself.

"DS Jones drug squad," the voice on the other end of the line said, "Morning David its Keith up in SCU," "Morning Keith, you old shirt-lifter, how's things going up in Serious Crime Unit?" "David one day you are going to say the wrong thing to the wrong person and either you will be on the wrong end of a beating or your fat arse will be marched out of the police force, and I for one wouldn't be sorry if that happened." "There's not a fag on this planet I wouldn't take on and whip their arse!!" "Before I come down there and do something you will regret, I need some info from you and your team about Tina Williamson, the girl that died in the house fire.

Also, about her family and friends including Ben Thorton." "I can't tell you too much, the whole family are small time players in shop lifting and minor drugs,

they do the odd bit of handling, but nothing we want to get involved with, too much time and paperwork to waste on getting nothing back in return as far as info or prosecution is concerned. As for Ben, why are you interested in him?" "His name cropped up in our team meeting and I know him from my uniform days and I was wondering if he was still on the scene or linked to the Williamsons?" DS jones thought about Ben for a moment and then thought of a way to get a bit more in the way of readies from Ben. "He is still about but is no longer involved with the family as far as we know." "Ok, if you can think of anything else which may help us, let me know." "No prob's, if you ever fancy going straight let me know and I will show you how a real man gets it done." "You have nothing to show me, I already know how a real man gets it done,

I have been married to my real man now for 12 years and we're still going strong." "Fucking poofter" Jones said slamming down the phone.

DS Jones picked up his mobile phone of the desk, found Ben's number and rang it. When the phone was answered DS Jones said "Benny boy, you have a problem and we need to meet up now,

be at the circle in 20 minutes and make sure you turn up." He cut the phone off before he could get a reply.

When Ben arrived at the circle, DS Jones was already there, "Where the hell have you been?" He asked, "Sorry 30, I'm only 5 minutes late." Well boy, you could be in a whole world of shit right about now, did you know that the queer queen in SCU is looking for you?"

"Me? Why what I have done?" Ben asked with a panic tone to his voice. "They are looking for you in relation to the murder of your Tina!"

"What the fuck do you mean murder; she died in the house fire!" "Oh no she didn't buddy boy, she died as a result of a slap or two, before the fire started. And you buddy boy are number 1 suspect. The colour from Ben's face got whiter by the second as all the blood drained from it. "With the colour of your face right about now, I am bloody certain you did have something to do with it." DS Jones laughed. But, but, but, Ben stammered "I didn't touch her!"

"Well that little speech tells me everything I needed to know!" DS Jones got right up into Ben's face,

"Right you little scumbag murderer, there is 2 ways we can go about this,

1/ I go to the SCU, and tell them everything I know about you and your little ways and basically hand you to them on a silver plate or

2/ You will give me 80% and I mean 80% of what you charge not 80% of the profit, and I will have very little weasel out there watching you and reporting back to me exactly what you are selling and who you are selling too. Plus, I want the name of the person who is supplying you the prescription drugs you have been selling and don't give me any bullshit you stole them from your family. So what option do you want Benny boy, if I didn't know already!" "80%? Ben gasped, 80% that would mean I would make a loss on everything I sold, unless I got it for free!" "Wow you catch on real fast, Benny boy, you either lose out to me or you spend the rest of your miserable drug addled life behind bars, in a stinky little prison cell, having god knows what done to you in the showers and as for the food, well if you like maggots, spit and anything else they want to put in food, then prison is the place for you. Oh, by the way, if you think you are going to just stop selling, I have another surprise for you, if 80% does not come up to £500 a week, you will just have to find the rest yourself, so may I suggest you fuck off and start selling or do you want to go down the SCU route.

To say that Ben did not know what had hit him, but if felt like a high-speed train had ran over his body. "30, please I'm begging you, I will do 80% of the profits but 80% of the sell price leaves nothing to buy anything with, please 30 don't do this, we have known each other a long time and you know I'm not a bad person, so I gave her a slap every so often, but that was just to keep her in place, you know what these women are if you let them get chopsy, they start taking liberties, but I swear I never slapped that hard she couldn't wake up again, I promise. I'm not a murderer, I'm not." "Ben, just fuck off out of my sight, and I will come and find YOU, next week for my money.

16

Carol woke up an hour before the alarm went off, after a very restless sleep, in fact she felt more tired now, then she did before she got into bed. She quickly picked up her phone to see if there were any messages from Ben, her heart sank when she saw no one had tried to ring her, let alone send her a text.

What should I do, she thought, should I text him? Should I ring him? In the end she decided to do nothing for an hour, as Ben might think I'm still asleep and he knows what time I get up when I'm on nights, maybe he will contact me then. If not, I will text him on the pretence of seeing if he is still going to take me to work.

Walking into the kitchen, she saw the bunch of flowers that Ben had brought her in the sink, she had forgot all about them, this brought a smile to her face and then if by magic the text notification went off on her phone and it was from Ben.

"My sexy Carol, forgive me for what I said in the car this morning, the pain at the moment is the worse pain I've ever experienced in my life and I don't know how to handle it. I will be at yours at 7.30 but I will understand if you don't want to get into the car. Love Ben. Ps hope you liked the flowers." Aww bless him, Carol thought, she text right back saying, looking forward to see you later and yes, the flowers are lovely, she ended the text with 3 kisses.

Dead on 7.30, Ben arrived at Carol's to take her to work. As she came out towards the car, Ben got out of his car and gave her a long kiss, "have we not got time for a coffee?" Ben asked. "Sorry hun, but I have to get to work, we have a team meeting, I promise to make up for it in the morning, if you want to pick me up." "Oh okay," Ben said dejectedly.

The drive to the hospital was in relative silence, neither one of them wanted to say the wrong thing and upset the other person.

About a half a mile from the hospital, Ben noticed blue flashing lights in his rear-view mirror, "Shit" he mumbled to himself, "I hope they are not after me." "Pardon hun, I didn't catch that," Carol said. "No, it's nothing, just remembered I needed to do something," he lied

The unmarked Police car pulled up alongside Ben, he was horrified to see it was Sergeant Jones. Sergeant Jones indicated for Ben to pull over. "Why are they stopping you Ben? Carol asked. "I hope it won't take long, as I don't want to be late for work." "Will you just shut up about bloody work!" Ben virtually shouted. What the hell was that all about? Carol thought to herself and decided not to say another word.

Ben pulled the car over to the kerbside and got out; he poked his head back through the door and told Carol to stay inside the car while he found out what the Police wanted. By the time Ben straightened up DS Jones was stood behind him.

"Get back in your car Benny boy." "Can't we talk outside or in your car?" Ben pleaded. "I'm sure you have nothing to hide from this pretty young lady, have you, Ben?" he said bending to look at Carol through the door.

DS Jones pushed Ben back into his car. Once again Ben muttered something under his breath, "What was that Ben? We didn't hear a word of it." DS Jones was really enjoying making Ben squirm in his seat. "You were supposed to come and see me, to give me something, weren't you Benny boy?" "But you said the end of the week!"

Ben said meekly, "Well I make the rules and you follow them and I have decided to make a point of catching up with you everyday, to make sure you give me what we agreed." Pushing his head into the car, DS Jones looked at Carol and said, "And who might you be young lady and what are you doing with this lowlife?" "I'm Carol Mcvitie, and I'm Ben's girlfriend and he is taking me to work, and as you can see by my uniform, I'm a nurse and I don't want to be late." "Sshh" Ben growled. "My, my, you have one with a voice, I bet that doesn't sit well with you, does it Ben, he usually likes his whores meek and quiet, don't you Benny!" "You maybe a Police officer but that doesn't give you the right to call me a whore!" Carol spat out. "The circle at 10 tonight and don't bring this little WHORE with you!" DS Jones said emphasising the word 'whore'.

With that DS Jones got back into his car and drove away. "What was that all about and why didn't you stick up for me?" Carol asked Ben. Ben's face was getting redder and redder with anger, then he snapped, "Just keep your fucking nose out of my business, he lifted his left arm swung it towards Carol, the back of his hand contacted Carol's right cheek, she recoiled with fright and pain, then burst into tears. It took about 5 seconds for Ben to realise what he had done.

Carol grabbed her bag and got out of the car screaming you will never see me again. She then started to walk the rest of the way to work. Ben just sat there trying to make sense of what had just happened. He thumped the steering wheel in anger and despair.

17

Carol went straight into the changing
rooms, when she got into work. When she
looked into the mirror she began to cry
again, the first stage of bruising was
showing on her cheek, her eyes were all
puffy from crying, just what have I got
myself into, she asked herself. Well that is
the last time he will ever lay a finger on me,
she sniffed. She washed her face, reapplied
her makeup, making sure she put plenty of
foundation powder on hoping it would
cover the oncoming bruise.

Coming out of the changing rooms, the
first-person Carol bumped into, was the last
person she was hoping to bump into, Jason.
"Can I see you in my office before we go
for handover." Jason asked. It was more of
an order then a request. Carol followed
Jason to his office. "Please take a seat,"
Carol sat opposite Jason. "Okay, you can
tell me to mind my own business and leave
the office at anytime you please, but I saw
you enter the hospital and I noticed you
were crying, now looking at you and the

fresh sign of a bruise is starting on your cheek, which by the looks of it you have tried to cover up with makeup.

Do you want to tell me what has happened?" Carol burst into tears again, "I'm sorry," she sobbed, but I must have upset Ben and he struck out." "What do you mean you must have upset him," Jason demanded to know. "We were driving along when Ben got stopped by the Police, a plains clothes officer came up to the car and started to have a go at Ben, he then demanded to know who I was, when I told him, he called me Ben's whore." "WHAT" Jason nearly exploded, "the Police officer called you a whore?" "Yes!" Carol cried. "Did you get his name?" "No, I didn't, and he isn't one that I have ever seen around the department." "Do you feel up to doing your shift?" Jason asked gently. "I will be okay, just give me time to tidy myself up, thank you." "Go and get yourself a coffee, come back to my office, sit in here for a bit, then come and find me in Resus." "Thank you, Jason, for understanding."

"Carol I never understand any man hitting a female, you know you don't have to put up with it, you can get Ben arrested for assault." "I know, but the thing is, that was his one and only time he will ever lay a hand on me, I've been through that before and I'm sure not doing it again, he is now out of my life and was the minute he raised his hand."

Jason stood up, and gave Carol a big hug, "You're a brave girl. Take your time, and if anyone asks you had some bad news on the way to work, but I would try to cover the bruise a bit more, or you will set the witches tongues wagging." He laughed.

Ben kept hitting his steering wheel as he drove away from the hospital, I have to come up with the most convincing lie ever, to get Carol back, he thought to himself. He drove back to his flat, grabbed the vodka bottle and took a massive swig, lit a cigarette, he turned his phone onto silent,

As he could think straight, without interruptions.

After a while, Ben had started to formulate a plan, but it would take a lot to pull it off, but it was all he had. It is time to put it all into action. Firstly, he checked his wallet, but was disappointed to find he only have a five-pound note in there. Shit, it all can't go wrong on the first step, He said out loud again to himself. Picking up his phone he took it off silent and rang Rob, "Hi Rob, you at home?" Rob said he was, "I will be at yours in 15 minutes. Ben drove as fast as he dared to Rob's. "Hi bud," Ben said as Rob opened the door.

"Rob, I need a massive favour, I know you said you weren't going sell your weed, but I'm in a whole fucking world of hurt, I need 6 ten bags, but I have only got a bluey on me, but you know I'm good for it. Please bud I really need you to help me out, or I'm going to get hurt big time." "I have only about 3 bags ready to go," Rob said. "That will get me started."

Rob reluctantly agreed to let Ben have the weed, even though Ben was a pain in the arse most of the time, he had helped him out in the past. Once he had the 3 bags, Ben drove back to his flat, where he ground up the weed in a small electric coffee grinder, searching under his bed, Ben found an old box, that had some old clippings from a plant he used to grow, until the cop's found it and took the plant away and leaving him with a £120 fine for the pleasure. Ben put the clippings into the grinder and ground them down with the other cannabis, emptying the ground up drugs into a bag, Ben realised he still didn't have enough for his plan to work. Bollocks, shit, wank, he said to himself angrily. I need to bulk this out, he said continuing to talk to himself. Then he remembered that his dad grew hemp in his garden which he used in fishing. Both hemp plants and cannabis plants look the same to the untrained eye while they are growing. Ben drove to his parent's house and was relieved to find they were not at home.

He let himself in with his key, which his parents didn't know he still had, grabbing a pair of scissors from the kitchen drawer, he headed out to his dad's greenhouse, Ben cut the heads off four plants and cut away some leaves as well. His dad would know instantly that his hemp plant had been cut up, but Ben didn't care, his dad would blame the local kids who would have thought it was a cannabis plant. Washing the scissors, he put them back into the drawer and let himself out of the house, doing a quick check to see if any of the neighbours had seen him. Getting back to his flat, he ground the hemp heads and leaves, he then added them to the bag of cannabis, giving them a good shake to mix up the contents.

Right, now to text Carol, Ben thought, this has to work, it's just got to work, or everything is screwed.

After writing the text, before sending it, he read it back to himself, "Hi Carol, there is no excuse for what I did, it shouldn't have happened, it was that the Police officer was frightening me and I took it out on you. Speaking to a friend, I have reason to believe that he wasn't the old bill at all. Just someone put up to it, who thought they would have a laugh at my expense. I am at Swindon police station right now, I have spoken to the detectives and they have said he wasn't a copper, I have also told them because of being frightened that I struck you, and they are going to send a Police officer to your house to check on you and to take a statement about what was said and done to you. If you want to press charges against me, I will not hold any grudges and I will accept any punishment that comes me way. Once again I'm sorry and if you never want to see me again I will understand Love Ben." She will fall for that hook line and sinker he smiled to himself.

Now the next part of my plan I need a bogus female Police officer and I know just the person and what it will cost me.

Picking up the bag of weed, Ben headed out again, this time to another dealer he knew dealt in crack cocaine rocks and was off his head most of the time he wouldn't realise what he was smoking.

He arranged to meet Steve in one of the pubs in the centre of Swindon. Steve was already there when Ben arrived with a pint of lager in his hand. Ben reached out to shake Steve's hand, "How's it hanging?" Ben asked, "To the left as always," laughed Steve.

"Steve, I have got a 75 bag of the best weed I have ever had, but a friend of mine is in need of some rocks, any chance you will do a deal with me?" "75 quid's worth of rocks is worth more than 75 quid's worth of green," "Do what?" asked Ben, "They are worth the fucking same you idiot, you've been smoking to many rocks yourself my friend." "NO, you get more weight in rocks for £75 then you would for £75 of green. Ben couldn't be bothered to argue you the point anymore, so he said, "I tell you what

Steve you give 50 quid's worth of rocks and I will give you the 75 quid's worth of green, that way you will be 25 quid up on the deal."

Ben could see that Steve was trying to work it out in his head, but being too stoned to work it out, then finally said, Yep I'll do that, let's go into the bogs and do the deal there.

In the toilet Steve shoved his hand down the front of his trousers and pulled out a plastic bag, which contained lots of little whiteish greyish rocks, from his inside pocket he pulled out a small set of scales and weighed out the right amount of rock's, but before handing them over to Ben he said "Put the green on the scales, I want to make sure you aren't trying to do me. Ben put the cannabis hemp mix onto the scales, Steve studied the figures on the scales, and said, "All good man," and passed the bag with the rocks in, over to Ben, "Nice dealing business with ya Ben, but my drink is calling me, so catch ya later man." They pumped fists and Ben walked out of the pub thinking to himself, now all I need is not to see a single copper between here and my flat.

Ben arrived at his flat without any incidents befalling him. Instead of going into his flat he went up 2 flights of stairs and knocked on the door. A middle aged dark haired, ever so slightly plump, woman answered the door, "Cassandra I need a huge favour, but I will more than make it worth your while." "Come on in "Cassandra said, "and tell me how I can help."

Once again Ben made up a whole bunch of lies about this that and the other but ended his story by asking if she would impersonate a WPC, to help him win his girlfriend back. "All I want you to do is to go there, pretend to be a copper, take a statement, you don't have to write down what she is saying, just make sure she can't see what you are writing, then say that I was very upset by what had happened and couldn't forgive myself, then ask if she wants to press charges against me.

Which I am pretty sure she will say she doesn't want too, and if she does, tell her you will be in touch then get out of there, I will get Rob to take you there and he will wait outside, then take you home afterwards and if you do this for me, you can have this, pulling out the bag of rocks, there is £60 worth there, if you agree then half now then half when we get back.

Cassandra's eyes lit up when she saw the rocks and agreed on the spot to help Ben out. Ben handed over half the rocks and said I will come and get you about 10 in the morning. As he walked back down to his flat he said to himself, Ben you are a fucking genius.

<u>18</u>

Carol spent the next 15 minutes sat in Jason's office; she couldn't understand why every man she dated; seemed to be a loser and thought it was okay to use her as a punch bag. She really hoped that Ben would be different, just once she would have loved, for her love life to have turned out to be perfect. She would have even accepted less than perfect, because everyone has their faults, just someone who loved her, cared about her, but more than that, someone who respected her.

She finished her coffee and thought to herself, okay put on a brave face, if anyone asks I will just say my aunty has been taken ill then change the subject. She then went back into the changing room, washed her face then applied some more foundation cream and changed into her scrubs.

Walking into the A&E department, no one seemed to be staring at her, as a matter of a fact, Lizzie, said laughing "Oh you are going to join us, boyfriend kept you in bed too long then?"

Then the normal humdrum of working in a busy A&E department swallowed her up and everything went into auto pilot.

A couple of hours later, Carol felt her phone vibrate in the pocket of her scrubs, even though she was busy, she sneaked a look at who it was, to her amazement it was Ben. She quickly put the phone away, thinking I leave that until my break.

All the cases coming in were run of the mill. Carol was stood at the corner of the desk waiting for a doctor to sign off on a patient's medication, when the red phone let out its loud shrill, as Carol was stood right next to it, the phone ringing made her jump, picking up the receiver she said, "Swindon Resus." "Good evening, this is Dr Clifford of the HEMS team, we are bringing you a male of approximate 65 years of age, a homeless gentleman who has gangrene in his right leg, which is oozing and smells really bad, and it is also infested with maggots, as is his foot. He has been drinking and is worse for wear; we can't get any accurate observations, as he is very combative. We have done a Rapid Sequence Induction for everyone's safety in the Helicopter; now he is asleep, he can't fight everyone. We will be with you in 18 minutes, can you have the helipad team ready for us please.

After writing everything down, Carol picked up the microphone and clearly said Adult surgical team to Resus, HEM'S ETA 18 minutes.

Twenty minutes later, the helicopter landed on the helipad. Carol was in the team waiting for the patient to be wheeled in. Have you got the buckets of warm water ready? Jason asked Carol.

"Yes, they are in the corner," she said pointing to the left-hand corner of the room. When the patient was wheeled into the bay, the smell coming from the patient's gangrenous leg, was overbearing, "Have we got any menthol rub available?" The consultant asked. Lizzie ran out to the desk, and came back with a tub of menthol rub, all the staff, placed a small amount under their nostrils, to help mitigate the smell. After the handover from the HEM's Doctor. The plastic's consultant removed the dressing from the patient's leg, to reveal a wound that was full of pus and maggots and what looked like pieces of clothing stuck to the dead and dying skin.

Carol could see Lizzie gagging beside the trolley, "Lizzie, do you want to go and check on the patient in Bay 2?" Carol asked. She gave Carol a look which said thank you so much; I would rather be anywhere rather than here.

"Ten milligrams of Diamorphine syringed, and can I have 15 more ready un-syringed!" The lead Plastic's called. Jason passed the keys to Carol, "Can you get that please." Carol went to the medicine cabinet and took out 5 x 5mg vials of Diamorphine; after checking the expiry date and lot numbers, she loaded two syringes, capped them, she couldn't find a little dish to put the other vial's in, so as not to keep the consultant waiting, she put the other 3 vials into her pocket, and made her way back to the Bay. She handed the consultant the first of the syringes, he also checked the expiry date and lot numbers, and then injected the patient directly into his leg, "This is going to have to come off," he said quietly to his registrar. "I will contact theatres and get them on standby," the registrar replied. "Make sure you inform them about the infestation, as the theatre will need a deep clean afterwards." "Yes sir." Came the reply.

Jason and Carol; started to undress the patient, when they took off his boot's; maggots were crawling between all his toes. Taking one of the buckets of warm water, they submerged one of the patient's feet into the water and watched as all the maggots fall off his foot and sink to the bottom of the bucket, "This is the quickest and cleanest way of getting rid of the maggots, so as we don't have them crawling all around the Resus room," he said. "God how I hate touching these bloody things," she said, "How fisherman do it, I don't know," she continued. They did the same with the other foot and got a porter to get rid of the buckets, "Don't just pour them down the sluice," Jason warned the porter, "dispose of them properly please." "I know just the person who will snatch my arm off for these," said the porter.

"What about the ones in his leg?" Carol asked. "We will leave that up to the theatre staff to work that one out." Jason Laughed.

"Carol, have you got the other syringe please," asked the consultant. Carol passed over the syringes, when the consultant passed the empty syringe back, Carol peeled off the little labels and stuck them onto the patient's drug sheet, so as there was a permanent record of how much diamorphine was used, when the patient received it and from what batch the medication came from.

After the patient had been taken off to theatre. Dr Anderson asked Carol for the remaining vials of diamorphine, "Do you want me to put them back into the drugs cabinet? Carol asked him. "No, I will do it!" The consultant said stiffly. Carol just shrugged her shoulders and handed the vials over. Jason told Carol and Lizzie to go on a break. They went off to the canteen together. On the way Lizzie was asking Carol how things were going with Ben. Carol didn't fancy going through it all with Lizzie, so she lied and said things were going well. This reminded Carol that she still had a text from Ben to read. After grabbing a coffee and a chocolate brownie, she sat down and read the text, she couldn't get her head around what she was reading, fake Police Officers, Ben handing himself into the Police for striking her, she needed someone to talk to about it, she thought about talking with Lizzie, but that would mean going back on what she had just said to her.

As soon as she had finished her coffee and half of her brownie, she excused herself, saying she needed the loo and had to speak to Jason about her off duty rota.

She found Jason sat in his office, entering, she asked him if he could spare her five minutes. "Of course, hun, take a pew, how can I help?" "After what happened earlier, Ben has sent me a text and I was wondering if you could read it and tell me what you make of it." "Yeah, no problem." Carol pulled up the message and passed her phone over to Jason. He read the message, then re-read the message, with a puzzled look on his face, he said, "do you find this message as weird as me?" "I do, that's why I asked you to read it." "I'm not sure if it is all made up and I suppose the only way you know if it is true, is if the police turn up at your place asking if you want to press charges against Ben. If it does turn out to be true, will you get back together with him?"

"That's my dilemma!" She said. "I am in love with him, even though we have only known each other five minutes, I really do have strong feelings for him, and Josh seems to like him as well, I really don't know what to do!"

"If it's true and the Police do turn up, it may be the only way of telling you whether or not to go with your heart or your brain." "Thank you, Jason, you have been a great help, and I really mean it." They both got up and Carol reached out and gave him a big hug and a kiss on his cheek. "Now get back to work before I fire your arse." Jason joked.

19

The serious crime unit got together in the small meeting room. DI Jamerson had called the meeting to see if any progress had been made in the Williamson case.

"Well, our main suspect Ben Thorton, has been cleared by the drug squad, as having nothing to do with the Williamson family for quite a while, even though he is still dabbling with low level drugs, so we have crossed him off, apparently Tina was in a relationship but with who, no one seems to know. In a nut shell we are no further forward then we were at the start. We have held off interviewing the family in depth until after the funeral. But as you would expect no one from the drug scene are talking, even our 'talkative friends'" He said making speech quotes in the air. "Have nothing to say." DS Keith Gregory said. "Well that's a whole lot of good news then!" DI Jamerson quipped.

"I can remember a time we could beat a suspect around the head until they talked to us." He laughed. "Sorry Inspector, but we have moved on from the Stone Age times, we have to get a health and safety assessment first now." DS Gregory quipped back.

"Seriously now," the DI said, "we have to find out who this boyfriend is and if he had any part in Tina's death. Someone out there knows something and I want to know as well.

DS Gregory returned to his desk with the file under his arm, placing it onto the table, the photo of Ben Thorton slipped out. Gregory stared at the picture, his gut was grinding, telling him something wasn't right, and this character had something to do with this crime even though the drug squad had cleared Thorton.

Meanwhile down in the drug squad offices, DS Jones was prowling around his office, he had lost track of Ben when he didn't turn up at the circle.

He had driven around all of Ben's regular haunts, asked a few of his friends, but the answer was the same, Ben had just vanished off the earth. "What the fuck are you up to, you snivelling little shit? When I got hold of you, you are going to regret crossing me!" he said to himself.

Ben was indeed in hiding, as there was no way he could find the sort of money 30 was after every day. Ben had driven down to his sister Anne's in Bridgewater in Somerset; he knew that there was no way that 30 would follow him down here and also not a lot of people knew him here either, so the chance of 30 finding out where he was, was very slim. Plus, Carol had not contacted him, which was pissing him off as well. Ben spent the day getting drunk and off his head on weed. About 8pm, he did something he was later to regret, he called his friend Rob. When he answered the phone, Rob said "Hi mate where are you? Been trying to see you, I called round to your place a couple of times,

I asked around, but no one knew where you were, and your mobile went straight to answerphone." "I had to get away to clear my head," Ben lied. "Will you be back in time for Tina's funeral on Thursday?" "I think the family might be pissed at me if I don't show my face, don't you think?" "True, so, where are you?" "I'm down in Somerset, at my sister's in Bridgewater." "Anyway Ben, I have to go, have a hot date with a big bag of green."

After hanging up the phone to Ben, Rob dialled a number and waited for it to be answered. "DS Jones," said as he picked up the call,

"30, I heard through the grapevine you are looking for Ben Thorton." "What if I am!" DS Jones said arrogantly. "Well I know where he is and when he will be back." Rob stated. "What's it worth for the information?" Rob asked, "Worth? I ought to throw your arse into a cell and leave you rotting there, but as I'm in such a good mood, I might be persuaded to accidently delete your arrest sheet, but let me warn you, if you are winding me up, your charges instead of being deleted will be tripled, do we understand each other?" "We sure do, Ben called me not 10 minutes ago, and he let it slip that he is staying at his sister's in Bridgewater and that he will be back for Tina's funeral on Thursday." "Consider your rap sheet wiped clean" DS Jones said and hung up the phone before Rob could say another word.

20

Carol ended her shift at the hospital and decided to walk home, to give herself some thinking time. She really didn't know what to do about Ben, overall, he was a really nice guy, he was funny, he made her feel important and he really knew how to treat a woman in the bedroom stakes. She had never had a man who made sure she was totally satisfied before satisfying himself.

After arriving home, she had made up her mind if the Police did turn up and confirm everything Ben had said, she was going to give him a second chance, even though it went against everything she believed in, the good in him outweighed the bad.

Carol had been home about two hours, when there was a loud knock on the door, "Carol McVitie?" "Yes" "I'm WDC Woods of Swindon Police, may I come in?" Carol showed the Detective Constable into her front room, they sat down opposite each other, Carol's first thought was thought woman was a bit old and scruffy to be a

Detective, but hey ho, undercover Police have to blend in she supposed. "Let me start, by asking you, do you know Ben Thorton?" "I do, up to recently we were in a relationship, but due to something that happened, we are no longer seeing each other." "That is why I have come to see you, he has done something that I rarely see, he came into the Police station and reported himself for hitting you. Now my questions are, 1: Did he attack you, if so, were you hurt in anyway? 2: If he did, do you want to press charges against him?" Carol was quite gob smacked that he had actually done what he said, it had left her with a warm feeling inside. "Yes, he did hit me, but it hardly touched me, she lied and no I don't want to press charges. I know it's still wrong, but if a man has the guts to own up to something he did and accept any consequences for doing it, he can't all be bad, and maybe he should deserve another chance, don't you think?" "If you are sure, we will leave it there and close the file, as long as you're really sure." "I am."

After the WDC had left, Carol called Jason, "Hi Jay" she said when he answered the phone, "You sound chipper," he said, "What's up?" "Well, I have just had a visit from the Police, and everything Ben said he had done, he actually had done, they asked if I wanted to press charges etc., I said I didn't. I think he deserves another chance,

what do you think?" "I think he has proven he can sort of be trusted, but I think you need to look at the bigger picture using your head and not your heart, take your time make sure it's what you want, that is my advice." "Thanks Jay, I will take my time, see you at work tomorrow."

The next day, Carol had made her mind up that she was going to contact Ben, but she would make him wait a few days, just to repay him for he had done to her.

Ben awoke the next morning, with a banging headache, and little recollection of what he had done the day before. Looking at his phone, he realised that he had called Rob. Oh shit, he thought to himself, what the hell did I say to him. If I said anything to drop me in it, I hope I can trust Rob not to say anything that could get back to 30. Ben thought about ringing Rob again but decided against it.

Carol walked to work the next morning feeling elated about what happened last night. Just as she walked up to the main entrance, she heard her name being called out.

She hoped it was Ben, but it turned out to be Jason, she stopped and waited for him to catch up. "Morning Jay," "Morning Carol, after chatting with you last night, I received another call, this was from the Matron, apparently they cannot account for 3 vials of diamorphine and I remembered that you only used 2 vials on the patient, what happened to the other three vials?" "Dr

Anderson asked me for them and so I gave them to him." "Okay I will let Matron know. Let's hope we have a 'Q' shift eh?" "Let's hope so."

After grabbing a big full English breakfast at a local café, Ben made his way through the rain, which hadn't stopped since he stepped outside earlier. Looking up to the sky as he walked along the pavement, there was nothing but grey skies and rain clouds, without realising it he walked into the road, and only became aware of it, when he heard a car blast its horn, Ben quickly looked ahead and saw that he was just inches away from the front of the car.

The driver wound down his window and started shouting abuse at Ben for not watching where he was going. Ben just stared at the driver, and then told the driver to go and fuck himself and went to walk away. The driver jumped out of his car and ran up to Ben, grabbing him by his collar, spun him around so that they were face to face, "What the fuck did you say to me, you asshole?" Ben replied, "I said go fuck yourself," pushing the driver away. Ben didn't see the driver throw his head forward until it was too late, as the man's forehead connected with the bridge of his nose. Ben fell backwards onto the road, hitting the back of his head hard of the road surface, then everything went black, as Ben lost consciousness.

When Ben came too, there was a paramedic hovering over him. "Lay still son," The voice said, "You have taken quite a blow to the back of your head and your nose seems to have taken a beating too. We are going to bandage you up and take you to Hospital." When the paramedic stood up, he was replaced by a Police Officer, "What happened?" he asked Ben. Not wanting to say what had really happened, Ben said that someone had tried to mug him, he had tried to fight him off, but he was far bigger then him. "Okay young man take it easy, we will talk to you more, once the doctors have worked their magic." Ben closed his eyes and drifted off to a place where everything was warm and cosy.

The next thing Ben remembered was being in a hospital bed, with a headache the size of Mount Everest, and a bandage wrapped around his head. Laying there, Ben thought to himself, why the fuck could nothing go right for him anymore. With that thought he closed eyes and drifted off to sleep.

21

The next few shifts passed very quietly for Carol, she hadn't heard anything from Ben. She thought to herself, I think he may have suffered enough now, so I will send him a text just asking how he is.

Ben was waiting to be discharged when he decided to turn on his phone, the phone chirped and bleeped, looking at the messages, he was delighted to see there was a message from Carol, he quickly opened it, it read, hi Ben how are you doing? He thought about how to reply, whether to mention the incident in his car. He wondered if the visit from the so called 'Police' had done the trick. In the end he decided to not mention it. The text he sent said, just leaving Bridgewater hospital, after being mugged, I have a broken nose and a large cut to the back of my head, which has 16 staples in it. But apart from that and my ribs from before, I am as sweet as a nut lol. After sending the text, Ben made his way back to his sisters to say his goodbye's then it was off back to Swindon.

When Carol received Ben's text, she was immediately concerned about him driving back to Swindon, she texted him right back saying that she finished work at 8pm and that he could he text her when he was back in Swindon. Ben agreed he would.

When Carol was in the changing room, Joanne the student nurse came in, "Hi Carol," Hiya Jo, How's the training going?" "I am finding it really hard, I know I have only been here for 10 weeks, but I still feel like a fish out of water." "Just hang on in there, keep your eyes and ears open and never be afraid to ask, 99% of the doctors will always give you an answer and will never treat you like you are stupid. What made you come into nursing?" "Well it was either this or the Police force, and nursing seemed the most interesting." "I know I would never swop nursing for any other job, after the years I have put in and the friends I have made, I don't think anything could replace the feeling you get, when a patient comes in near to death, then before you know it they are walking out of the hospital completely healed." "So how do you get on with the top doc's?" Joanne asked, "me? Really good, when I first started in nursing some of the older consultants had a superior god complex, but times have changed and now the look on us as equals, and some even treat us better than their juniors." "What about other members of the team, do you ever cover for each other?" Carol gave Joanne a look which said, why are you asking me these sorts of questions? "Sorry" said Joanne, "It just seems like I can't seem to fit in and was wondering if it was the same for everyone when they first start their training." Still unsure of what Joanne was trying to get at, Carol just smiled and continued getting changed.

Carol was just approaching the desk when the red phone rang, Carol reached out and answered the call, "Swindon Resus," "Good morning, we are bringing you a 76-year old male, who fell off his toilet, his right foot bent back so far that he has an open fracture and his foot is only being held on by a small amount of skin. We will be with you in approx. 8 minutes." Carol announced over the tannoy that a male trauma will be arriving in 8 minutes. "Joanne, can you go and get bay 2 ready for this patient?" Carol asked. 8 minutes later the ambulance crew wheeled in the patient. "Eugh" exclaimed Joanne, when the patients wound was revealed. "How the heck did he manage to do that?" she asked Carol, "apparently he went to stand up from the toilet, he over balanced and his foot went backwards underneath him, then the weight of his body pushed the tib and fib through the skin, so his foot was facing backwards with the bones sticking out of the bottom of his leg just above the ankle, not that you would know he has such a major injury, he said he didn't want any pain killers at all. The paramedic said if it was him, he would be screaming his head off."

Ben arrived back in Swindon and texted
Carol to let her know he was back. Carol
text back and said he could pick her up
from work, when she finished around 8 that
evening, if he wanted too? The rest of
Carol's shift was very busy, and the time
flew by, before she knew it, Jason was
saying, "that will do now girls, run away
while the Resus is empty" Carol didn't need
telling twice, she was very apprehensive
about meeting up with Ben again, "You can
do this," she said to herself. "Things will
work out, it will be alright," she tried to
convince herself. Walking outside, she
didn't see Ben's car straight away, "Oh he
hasn't come," she thought. Then a car
moved away and there was Ben's car, he
was sat inside, but as soon as he saw her,
Ben got out and stood next to his car.

As she approached him, she could see the
plaster across the bridge of his nose, and the
bruising around both eyes, "OMG" she said
"look at the state of your face" she said to
him. "I thought it actually improved my
looks," Ben Laughed. "Yeah I can see that,"

she joked back. They got into the car and Ben drove them to Carol's. When they arrived, Ben just sat in his seat with his seatbelt on, "Do you not want to come in?" Carol asked. "If you are sure, I would love to come in."

22

DS Keith Gregory had been working
tirelessly on the Tina Williamson's case. He
had interviewed everyone he could. He
wanted to re-interview members of her
family, because it had come to a point
where he couldn't move forward until he
had spoken to them again, as something
wasn't making sense. The drug squad had
cleared Ben Thorton, but everyone he had
spoken too, was saying then Ben WAS! still
involved with Tina, up and to the point of
her death, not only that, one of Tina's
neighbours had stated that he had seen
Ben's car outside of Tina's house on the
day of the fire.

He decided to take it to the DI. "Morning
boss," "Morning Keith, how's the
Williamson case going?" "Call it a copper's
nose, but something just isn't right on this
one, I spoke with DS Jones, in the drug
squad, and he vouched for Ben Thorton, but
everyone I have spoken to seems to think
that he was still in a relationship with the

deceased when she died." "What are the family saying?" "When I first spoke to them, bearing in mind they were grieving, none of them actually said Ben was in a relationship with Tina, but they also didn't say he wasn't," "Okay" the DI said, "I want to speak to them again, but with the funeral on Thursday, so I thought I would ask you whether or not I should wait until afterwards." "No, I think you should speak to them as soon as possible; I am sure they are as keen to find out the truth about what happened as we are." "Ok boss, I will do it today, check in with you later."

Later that same day, DS Gregory, made his way to the Williamson's home. On arrival the only person home was the son, Stuart. "Hello Stuart, I am DS Gregory of Swindon Police," he said showing Stuart his warrant card. "Yeah what do you want," came the curse reply. "Can you tell me about Ben Thorton, what was he to Tina and this family?" "What do you mean, what was he to Tina? He was her partner, Why?" "when you say was, how long ago did they split up?" "Split up? They hadn't split up; they were together right up to the time my sister died."

"Not that I don't believe you, but are you really sure, as we have it on very good authority that Ben and Tina were no longer together and haven't been for quite a while."

"Well I don't know who is telling you this crap, but I know for a fact that they were still together and seeing as we're family we would be the first to know if one of them had dumped the other one." "Thank you, Stuart, before you go can I ask another quick question," Was Ben handy with his fists towards your sister?" "Once again, why are you asking me these sorts of questions?" "Stuart have you or your family read the Coroner's Report?" Gregory said, knowing full well that neither Stuart or his mum and dad could read or write, Tina was the one who had had some schooling and took care of any paperwork that needed taking care of. "My dad has," Stuart lied, "but he didn't seem to really understand it. Why; what did it say?" "Well nothing much more than we expected, except for one thing, it said Tina had been hit very hard just before she had died, and because she was unconscious at the time of the fire, there was no way she could have got out."

Stuart jumped out of his chair, his face red with anger, "do you mean my sister was MURDERED?" he shouted out. "Stuart" DS Gregory said in a soft voice trying to calm Stuart down, "That is what we believe and that's is the line of enquiry we are conducting at the moment." Stuart exploded again, "I will fucking kill that scumbag,

I swear I will." "No, you won't Stuart, who will look after your mum and dad if you are spending the rest of your life in prison?" "I don't fucking care, I want to hurt him so bad just like he hurt my sister." "Stuart, we don't know it was Ben, he could be totally innocent, leave it to us to find out the truth about what happened and who has committed this act." Stuart mumbled something under his breath, "I need you to leave now, mum and dad will be back soon, and I want to talk to them by myself." "Okay Stuart, I will go, but remember what I said about spending the rest of your life in prison, lets us do our job, we are good at it and we will find out what happened and bring the culprit to justice the legal way, not the angry mob way."

With that warning, DS Gregory left. He couldn't have been halfway down the path, before Stuart was on the phone to his parents.

As hard as he tried he couldn't get his dad or his mum to pick up the phone, by the 5th time of trying, he could feel his anger rising, then finally his dad answered his phone, "Why the fuck don't you answer your phone," Stuart shouted," but before his dad could answer, he carried on, "where are you?" "you know where we are, we are in town," "No idiot where are you right now?"

Mr Williamson explained where they were,
right meet me at the café on Havelock
Street in half an hour and don't be late."
"What the hell has bit your arse son?" but
he was talking to himself, as Stuart had
hung up the phone.

23

Ben and Carol were driving along when Ben turned to her and lied, "I need to tell you the truth." Do you remember when we first met, I told you that I was beaten up by four strangers, well that wasn't true, I did know them, they were drug dealers and because the Police are clamping down on drugs getting into Swindon, the dealers are trying other ways to get their drugs and one of the ways they are doing it, is by stealing other peoples prescribed medication or making people steal medication with the threat of violence if they don't get them any, and because once I was desperate for money I sold them some of my medication and have regretted it ever since, they even tracked me down to my sisters in Bridgewater and attacked me there." "But why haven't you gone to the Police?" "I have, I spoke with someone from the drugs squad, whose name I can't remember" he lied again, "he promised to look into it and help get these men off my back but what I didn't know was he was in the pocket of the criminals and nothing ever came of my case."

The lies just rolled off his tongue and it seemed that Carol was taking it all in. "You have really been unlucky, but this does leave me with a problem, I can't put myself or my son at any risk of getting mixed up with these sort of people." "I promise you those men will never know who you are, where you live or even if you are in a relationship with me, but I really do need your help in getting medication, because as long as I am supplying them, then they won't need to hurt me." "I don't know Ben, this all seems very dangerous and frightening to me." "If you do help me, I will make sure nothing ever happens to you or little Josh 'EVER'." For the rest of the journey to Carols place, the conversation was very strained with long bouts of silence. When they arrived at Carols, she turned to him and said, "Listen I need to think this through, if you don't mind I will spend the evening thinking about it and I will text or call you later." "Okay, I would have loved to spend the evening with you, but I do understand you need time to think it all through. Please promise to either text or call me later." She promised she would and went indoors.

Once indoors, Carol put the kettle on, made herself a coffee and a sandwich and was about halfway through it when the doorbell rang out. Carol was surprised when she opened the front door to her mum and son. "Hello mum, wasn't I coming round to yours to pick little man up," She said scooping her son up into her arms and planting a huge kiss on him, Josh responded by squeezing her neck with his little arms. "Josh wanted to come home early, so we decided to take a little walk and a bus ride and meet you here, and why is the kettle not on yet?" Carol made her mum a cup of tea, all the while answering hundreds of questions asked by Josh, why is this, why is that, nanny said this, nanny said that, but it was what he said last, that made Carol smile the most, he said "Mummy I love you." "I love you too sweetpea." She replied.

24

When Stuart reached the café, his parents
were already there. The café was nearly full
with customers. He pulled out the chair
opposite his father and sat down, "What
have you got a bee in your bonnet about
son?" Stuart took a deep breath, "You know
that report that you got about how Tina
died, well a copper called Gregory or
something like that, just called at the house
and said that our Tina was murdered,"
"What do you mean murdered," he said in a
very loud voice, so loud in fact the whole
café went silent, one chap sat on the next
table eating his lunch, stopped with his fork
halfway to his mouth. Stuart turned around
and stared at the other customers and
shouted, "Mind your own fucking
business!" The three of them huddled closer
together to try and keep the conversation as
private as they could. "Right son tell me
from the very beginning what happened."
"As I said this copper turned up at the door
wanting to speak to you or mum, anyway I
told him that you were both in town,

He asked if he could ask me a couple of questions," "AND" his father said, "Give me a fucking chance and I will tell you, he asked me if we had read and understood the report the coroner had sent you.

I said you had, but I knew you hadn't, he went on to say did we realise that Tina had been beaten up so bad before the fire that she was unconscious when the fire started and that she didn't have a chance to get out." "Oh no not my little Tina." Mrs Williamson cried out. "Mum that's not all, the copper then asked me if Ben and Tina were together at the time she died as he had heard they had been split up for ages. He also asked me if Ben was handy with his fist's where Tina was concerned. The way he was talking even though he didn't actually say the words to me, but it seemed he was saying that Ben murdered her!" "Oh no, not our Ben" she cried out, once again the café fell silent. This time Stuart stood up and shouted out "I thought I told you all to mind your own fucking business.

Come on let's get out of here away from these nosey shits." "Alright, I will just pay." "Fuck no are you going to pay, and if they don't like it they can come outside and deal with me."

With that the family got up and left the café, the owner thought about going after them, but thought better of it, he knew the family and would just add it to their bill next time they came in.

Outside the family stopped and all lit cigarettes. "I am going to break every bone in his skinny little body until I find out the truth and then if it is true, it will then be the last minute of his life." Mr Williamson said. "No dad, that copper said if anything happened to Ben, we will be the ones that end up in jail, but don't worry about it, he will get what's coming to him even if it's at the funeral tomorrow.

Carol spent what seem like hours thinking repeatedly about what Ben had told her. I need to go somewhere and clear my head, she thought to herself, so I can make the decision that is right for me and Josh. Just then an idea popped into her head, she reached for her phone and dialled a number from her contacts list. When the phone was answered she said "Hello aunty Linda, how are you and how is the lovely Isle of Wight?

"Carol it's so nice to hear from you, it's been ages since we spoke, how are things with you?" "Well that's the reason for the call, I was wondering if Josh and I could come over for a few days?" "My darling, I would be delighted if you were to come over, when are you thinking of?" "I have the next five days off work, so we could come over tomorrow for 3 or 4 days, if that is not too short of a notice." "Of course not, would you be sailing from Southampton or Portsmouth?" "Southampton, as it's easier to get a train there then Portsmouth, also the boat ride is an hour long and Josh loves being on the boat." "Well you let me know what time your sailing is, and I will get Baz to pick you up from East Cowes." "Thank you so much aunty Linda. See you some time tomorrow."

After finishing her call with her aunty, Carol picked another number from her contacts list, this time it was Ben she was calling. "Hiya," she said when he answered, "Hiya yourself, I am so glad you call, to be honest I didn't think you would call, I was expecting a 'Dear John' text'." "No, I have given it some thought, I think we may be able to get over this, but I want to think about it some more, so I have decided to go too my aunties on the Isle of Wight for 4 days, I am going to go over tomorrow from Southampton."

"I would offer you a lift down there, but I have Tina's funeral tomorrow." "Oh, I am so sorry, I had forgotten you had that to go too, maybe it's a good thing that I am going away, as it might have put some unwanted pressure on us, when that's the last thing we need at the moment, don't you agree?" "Yes and no, I would have liked the company afterwards, but if you were not sure about us, then me spending the night with you could ruin things." "Hey who said anything about you spending the night?" Carol laughed. "No seriously, if this is going to work we both have to be 100% sure it's what we want." "Okay but can I call or text you over the next few days?" "Text's will be alright, but I think calls may interfere with my thoughts." Ben reluctantly agreed, and Carol ended the call.

Well Benny boy, things seem to be getting back on track, just a whole load of shit to sort out, then I can go back to being who I want to be. He thought to himself.

25

The morning of Tina Williamson's funeral was grey and overcast with the occasional rain shower, Inter-mingled with the mourners were 4 undercover Police Officers from the Serious Crime Squad, on the lookout for Ben Thorton, with orders to arrest him for any reason they could even if it was Section 5 public order disturbance.

Stuart stood at the kitchen window keeping a lookout for Ben also, but for a totally different reason. Just as the funeral cars arrived, the hearse carrying Tina's coffin followed by 1 other black limousine, Stuart spotted Ben walking up the road, he flew out of the kitchen heading for the front door, Mr Williamson made a grab for Stuart's collar, managing only to rip his jacket. As Stuart ran up to Ben, he swung his right fist and connected with the side of Ben's face, sending Ben to the floor while screaming "YOU KILLED MY SISTER YOU BASTARD!" All the mourners stopped what they were doing turned and stared at Stuart who was kicking Ben on the ground.

Ben managed to get to his feet and head-butted Stuart just as the Police Officers ran in to separate the fighters.

As soon as they were pulled apart, DC Clarke stepped forward and handcuffed Ben informing him that he was under arrest for causing a public disorder, he read him rights then pushed him into the back seat of an unmarked Police car. Turning to Stuart he said "If it wasn't for your sister's funeral you would be joining him in custody. Don't think you have got away with anything, I will be back to arrest you tomorrow, unless you turn up at the Police Station by 10am, on your own accord." "Just get that bastard away from here, before the crowd turn nasty," Stuart said angrily. "Go back inside before I change my mind and take you to the nick as well." DC Clarke said.

Stuart sulked off back into the house, "What the hell do you think you were playing at?" His father asked.

"As soon as I saw him the red mist came down and I couldn't help myself, I just wanted to hurt him for hurting this family."
"Yeah, but what if the Police are wrong and Ben had nothing to do with Tina's death?

You will end up going to prison for attacking an innocent man BUT believe me IF Ben had something to do with it, he won't be walking this earth much longer.

Go and get my spare jacket out of my wardrobe, as you can't go looking like that." The rest of the funeral went off without any other incidents except for Mrs Williamson screaming out Tina my Sweet, sweet Tina. The wake was being held in a local pub. People who were not at the house and didn't see what went on between Stuart and Ben but had heard that something had gone on between them, were coming up and asking what had taken place and also why had the Police been asking questions about Ben and why wasn't he here at the wake. The more people that said they had been asked about Ben by the Police, the more convinced that the Williamson's became that Ben did have something to do with Tina's death. By the end of the evening a very drunk Mr Williamson had declared that he would be going to prison soon as he going to kill Ben the moment he found him.

Meanwhile at Swindon's main Police station, Ben had been through the custody procedures and placed in a cell.

DC Clarke was reporting to his boss DS Gregory. He reported how Stuart had attacked Ben and that he had just heard that the Williamson's were now certain of Ben's guilt and that they were now out to harm him as soon as he is released. "Okay let's leave Ben to stew overnight in his cell, then you and I will interview him in the morning and see where it will take us, you never know he just might put his hands up to it and save us all a lot of hassle." "Boss if that happens, I will be going to church every Sunday morning." DC Clarke said sarcastically.

Carol had made it safe and sound to her aunties on the Isle of Wight. After settling Josh down in bed, Carol and her aunty sat at the kitchen table with a steaming cup of hot chocolate, while her uncle sat in the front room watching the football. "My favourite darling niece, what brings you scampering over the Solent?" "Man trouble, aunty Lyn man trouble." "Come on then, let's hear all about it." Carol told her all about Ben, what had happened in the car, then the business with the Police and how he made her feel inside etc. "Well my opinion sweetie is if a man is capable of hitting a woman once,

he is more than capable of hitting out again, I've always said no man would ever get another chance with me, if he hit me or cheated on me, you see enough of these sort of men on a very well-known morning program and the women who are used as punch bags all in the name of love, you don't want to end up on that show, battered black and blue and pleading for help." "I know what you are saying Lyn, but something inside of me tells me this one is different, the fact that *HE* went to the Police is what has swayed it for me, I'm going to give him another chance, but believe me if he even raises a hand towards me he will be out of my life faster than you can say 'All nurses are super human beings with the patience of the saints'," "Well you are old enough, I'm not going to say ugly enough, because you are one pretty young lady, but you make your bed and you lay in it. Of course, I wish you all the best and I really hope it all works out for you and Josh, as you deserve some happiness and I suppose there must be another Baz out there, or have I got the only decent gentleman left in England." "Just you wait until you pop your clogs I will be in there like a shot." Carol laughed.

26

Ben spent a sleepless night in the Police cells. He had only just dropped off when he heard the keys go into the lock and the duty Sergeant entered the cell, "Ben John Thorton, you are also being held in the connection of the death of Tina Williamson, alongside the Section 5 charge. If you now think you require a solicitor I can arrange the duty solicitor to come and see you or if you have your own I will contact them. Whereas last night you declined one, I am now giving you the opportunity to seek legal representation before you are interviewed, if you decline, I will let the officers dealing with you that you are ready to be interviewed. Do you require legal representation?" "Yes, can you get hold of Ross Robb for me?" "How did I know you were going to ask for him? The duty sergeant said with a smile. "Yeah well, he has always looked after me, so off you trot and get him here, you can tell the muppets upstairs that I won't be talking to anyone until Ross is here and I have had a chance to talk with him." "Whatever big man," came the reply and the cell door slammed shut with a loud clanging noise.

An hour later Ross Robb arrived at Swindon Police Station, walking up to the charge room desk, he asked if he could see his client Ben Thorton. The duty sergeant greeted Ross warmly, "Morning Mr Robb how are you today?" "What has my client been brought in for?" totally ignoring the Sergeant. "Ben Thorton was originally brought in under section 5. The SCU now want to interview Mr Thorton in relation to the death of one Tina Williamson." The Sergeant said in a very business-like manner due to being pissed off that Robb couldn't be bothered with any pleasantries. "I would like to see my client now," Robb demanded. The Sergeant directed him into a side interview room saying that he will get his client as soon as he could, then went off to get a coffee. Thirty minutes later the Sergeant went and got Ben from his cell and escorted him to the interview room, opening the door, he apologised for the length of time it had taken to bring the prisoner to Robb, but this was due to an urgent call.

"What the hell is this all about?" Ben demanded to know," First of all I get attacked, next thing I know 3 burly coppers jump on me and tell me that I am being nicked for breach of the peace, they throw me in the cell, keep me over night then when I wake up they tell me I'm being questioned about the death of my ex-partner." "Calm down, tell me from the beginning what happened when it happened and how it happened," Ross Robb said. "As I said, I just arrived at Tina's parent's house, to go to Tina's funeral and to pass on my condolences, When Stuart flew out the house and jumped me, sending me flying into the road, I managed to get to my feet in spite of Stuart trying to kick the fuck out of me, I retaliated by head butting the little shit, next thing I know the cops pounced on me, telling me I'm nicked. Then as I said they tell me this morning I going to quizzed about Tina's death." "Who pounced on you? PC Plod? Plain clothes CID? Who? And who told you about being interview and who are you to be interviewed by?" "The duty sergeant told me about the interview and it was plain clothes who jumped on me." Ben then explained everything that happened from the time he turned up at the house, right up to being brought into the room for the interview. "Are you hurt or in pain?" "Too bloody right I'm in pain!" In that case I will insist you are taken to the hospital for a check-up and it will give us more off a chance to talk before they get going on you."

Carol was really enjoying herself at her aunties, it was the first time in ages she was able to relax with Josh and she could tell by the smile on his face he was enjoying it too, or maybe being spoilt rotten by Lynn and Baz was the real reason he was smiling the whole time. Lynn noticed that Carol kept glancing down at her phone. "Are you expecting him to call?" "No" replied Caro, l "I was hoping for a text, but I guess he is trying to do the right thing and give me the space I asked for, I suppose I wanted my cake and eat it," Carol laughed. "My darling niece, men are creatures of habit, he will contact you, of that you can be sure. Just remember in this day and age, we women rule the roost, we say jump and they ask how high, the secret is not to ask them jump too high." "Auntie Lynn you are incorrigible, you really are, how Baz has put up with you for all these years I will never know." "Baz thinks he wears the trousers in this relationship, but I tell him which ones to wear. No honestly our secret is we give, and we take, and we talk, but most of all, we are each other's best friend and it is as simple as that." "I really hope one day I can say that to my son with Ben by my side."

After being checked over at the A&E Dept. And being giving the all clear to interviewed Ben was returned to the Police Station. DS Gregory prepared the interview room ready for Ben's interview. Turning to his DC he said, "I bet you a fiver that we get an 'No Comment' interview." "I think that would be a mug's bet, Sarge."

Ben and his solicitor entered the interview room and sat opposite DS Gregory and DC Roberts. The DS put a CD into the recording machine and announced who was in the room. "Okay Ben, we are interviewing you in relation to the death of Tina Williamson, would you like to save us all the time and effort and admit that you were responsible for Tina's death." Expecting a 'no comment', Ben said "No." The DS waited for the next word 'comment' but it didn't come, this caught the DS off guard a little, but he soon recovered and came back with "No, you don't want to save all our time or what?"

Ross Robb advised Ben that he didn't have to answer the question, but before he had finished Ben was shouting at the DS, "NO I DIDN'T KILL TINA!" "I didn't say that you killed her, I asked whether you are responsible for her death." "What do you mean responsible?" Ben demanded to know. "Did any actions by you lead to Tina's death?" "Of course not, why would I have anything to do with her death, I loved her, I wouldn't harm a hair on her head. He said with a smug look on his face. "So she dumped you then Ben?" DS Gregory saw Ben's face go from white too bright red with anger. Ross Robb turned to the detectives and asked if they had any evidence at all that linked his client to the murder of Tina Williamson, if not he insisted that his client be released immediately and as for the other matter of the public order offence that should be dealt with by the way of a Police caution.

DS Gregory, glanced at his colleague, DC Roberts gave a little shake of his head, as if to say, we have nothing boss and we can't pursue it any further at this point. DS Gregory reached over switched off the recording machine, removed the CD, placed it into its cover signed the back of the attached form and passed it to Ben to sign it as well. After Ben had signed the form, DS

Gregory informed Ben he was free to go on this matter, but the desk sergeant would make the decision in relation to the section 4 offence. He also informed him that at any time new evidence came to light about the death of Tina, Ben would be brought in again. Ben replied "Yeah, whatever."

DC Roberts led Ben and Ross back to the charge desk, after explaining to the sergeant what was happening, the sergeant informed Ben that he was giving him an official warning about his conduct in public places and what would happen if he was to return to the Police Station in the next 12 months on the same charge. Once again Ben replied with "whatever." The Sergeant looked directly at Ben and said, "Go on piss off out of here before I nick you for being a complete waste of a human being." Ben turned around started to walk out but stopped after a few steps and looked back at the desk and gave a one finger salute to the desk Sergeant.

27

After being released from police custody, Ben was unsure of where to go, he was worried if he returned to his flat or to any of his usual haunts, word would get back to the Williamson's and they would come after him. He couldn't go to Carol's either as she was over on the Isle of Wight, with her family. He thought about going back to Bridgewater, but once again he was worried that someone would spot him, perhaps he was safer in the Police cells he thought to himself. He needed to charge his phone as well, so at least he could make some arrangements, as it was totally dead. If he could get to his car, which was still parked outside Tina's, without being spotted, he could use his car charger. He decided to chance by catching the bus to Tina's but get off a few stops early and walk the rest of the way. Then he could watch his car from a distance, just to make sure that the Williamson's hadn't got people watching his car, or had it disabled in some way.

After a quick bus ride, he walked slowly towards his car, his head turning left and right, taking in everything that was going on around him, it was his own good fortune that it was a very cloudy day and there was not a lot of people on the streets. Finally, his car came into sight. Ben slowed his walking down to a crawl, he looked at every window as he passed it to see if he was being watched. So far so good, just as he reached the car, a door opened, and a woman came out, "Hi Ben," she said "How are you? Stuart was looking for you earlier." "Yeah I know, I spoke to him a little while ago," he lied. "I just going around to his house now," he lied again. Before she could answer, Ben got in his car, started his car and drove away squealing the tyres in the process. He quickly drove to the other side of the town in a bit of a panic to an industrial estate, where he stopped the car and took a deep breath and tried to calm himself down. He plugged in the phone charger and waited while it charged enough so as he could switch the phone on. He smoked a cigarette while he waited, it also helped calm him down.

After a few minutes he was able to turn on his phone and just as quickly messages and missed calls started appearing on his screen. The one message he wanted to see was indeed there. He quickly opened it and as he read the content, for the first time in ages a smile came across his face. The message was from Carol, telling him that not only was she at home, she couldn't wait to see him, so she came home a day early. She also thanked him for keeping his word in not harassing her whilst she was at her aunties. At long last, I've managed to catch a break, he thought to himself. Right, now I have to turn this all to my advantage he continued to think to himself. I need to persuade Carol to allow me to stay at hers for a while. He sat there in his car thinking how he could achieve everything he needed to achieve. Finally, he had a clear plan of what he had to do, first he would risk going to his flat once it was dark and collect whatever belongings and clothes he could fit into his car with one visit. He would then check into a cheap hotel overnight, then in the morning he would turn up at Carols at blag his way into her letting him stay, by using the excuse he had been evicted and had nowhere to live except the back of his car, all because he had had his bank account hacked and the hacker had taken everything he had in the world.

As soon as it was dark enough, he put his plan into action. He drove and parked close to his flat, sitting watching the area around his flat, checking to see if anything suspicious was going on. Once he was satisfied all seemed clear, he crept the car along the road without any headlights on, until his was outside his flat. He turned off his interior light, so it wouldn't show when he opened the car door. Once out of the car, he walked briskly to his front door, before opening it, he placed his ear against it to listen for any noise coming from inside. Satisfied he couldn't hear anything, he quietly put the key into the lock and opened the door, stepping inside he was not surprised to see that his flat had been turned over. With the light from his phone, he made his way into his bedroom, grabbing a black sports holdall, he stuffed as many clothes into it as he could, he also put in his phone charger and tablet charger, and his electric shaver. He opened the wardrobe door pulled out the plinth and reached in and pulled out a washbag. Thanking his lucky stars, whoever had turned his flat over had not found his hiding place. Inside the bag was a bundle of notes held together by an elastic band and bag of pills, stuffing the money into his pocket and putting the pills into his bag he made his way into his bathroom, picking up his toothbrush, he reached behind the toilet bowl, stuck to the back was an envelope containing a bundle of notes, putting this into his pocket as well, he made his way into the kitchen, opening a cupboard door he reached in and pulled out a box of cereal, emptying the contents onto the work surface amongst the cereal was more notes bound by another elastic band, pocketing these he then opened the kitchen sink cabinet, taking out a box of washing powder, he also emptied this out and inside wrapped in a plastic bag was some more tablets and powders. Taking some shopping bags with him, he then went into the living room. As hard as he looked in the living room, he could not find his tablet anywhere, cursing his luck on that, he grabbed some DVD's and CD's and a couple of photo's, shoving them all into the bags, he made his way back to the front door, stopping to grab a couple of jackets off the coat hooks, he left the flat, making sure to close the door as quietly as he could. Just as he was closing the boot, he noticed the curtains in the house opposite twitch. Time to get the hell out of here, Ben said to himself. Starting the engine, he drove away with the lights switched off until he turned the corner. Breathing a huge sigh of relief, he made his way to the outskirts of town to a hotel, where he checked in under a false name, paying for the room upfront in cash.

While in the shower he heard the message tone coming from his phone, throwing a towel around his wet body he went back into the bedroom and picked up the phone, it was a message from Carol, letting him know that she was thinking about him and that she was just getting into bed because as she had come back early, she was going to do an extra early shift. Ben messaged back saying that he wished he was with her right now but understood about having to get up early and asking could the meet up tomorrow when she came off duty. He waited what seemed like ages for the reply but actually it was only a minute. Carol said that she couldn't wait to see him and if he wanted he could pick her up from the hospital, and that she would text him during the morning. She wished him goodnight and ended the message with a fair few kisses. Ben messaged her goodnight and after counting the kisses he made sure he ended the message with more kisses then she had sent.

28

DS Gregory arrived for work an hour before he was supposed to. He wanted to make sure he had covered all the bases covered, dotted all the I's and crossed all the T's in his report before the morning brief. He knew the DI would not be happy with how the interview with Ben Thorton had gone. He also knew that he had nothing else to offer in relation to Tina Williamson's death.

A couple of hours later, everyone from the Serious Crime Squad was gather in meeting room A. The DI called the meeting to order, "Good morning all, it's been a busy couple of days and hopefully we have had some good results! We will start with DS Gregory, okay Keith what good news have you got for me?" "I'm afraid Sir, I have nothing but bad news. We interviewed Ben Thorton and we got absolutely nothing, now I know he did it, Tina's family knows he did it, as a matter of a fact most people know he did it, but we just can't prove it. We have not a shred of physical evidence, no forensic evidence and no-one will say a damned word about it.

Now Ben Thorton is no 'Big Boss' everyone fears, he is just about as scary as my ginger tom cat, but someone out there is pulling the strings and putting the frighteners on Joe public to keep their mouths tightly shut." The DI looked at DS Gregory with a look that could kill. "What the hell went on in that interview room that ended with Thorton walking out this building?" "Sir, as I said we haven't got any concrete evidence it is all circumstantial and hearsay and with Ross Robb picking away at what little we do have, there was no option but to let him go." "Tell me about your views on this 'Mr Big' then Keith?" "Once again, this is what is really puzzling my team, we have never come across or even heard of a person who could weld that sort of influence over the criminal classes in Swindon." "Then you need to dig deeper to identify this person. What about other departments, have you asked around if they have any information on this 'Mr Big'?" "I haven't, but that is on my list of things to do today." "Have you written up your report on the interview Keith?" "Yes Sir, you will have it on conclusion of this meeting." "Good in that case, let's move on to the next item," the DI concluded.

Ben had woken up feeling relaxed for the first morning in ages. He made his way down to the hotel's restaurant and enjoyed a full English breakfast. Getting back to his room, he sent Carol a good morning text, which she replied to straight away. Emptying the sports bag and the contents of his pockets onto the bed, he discovered he had just over £5000 in cash and another grand in drugs that he could sell. Not that he would let Carol know of course, because as far as she was concerned he was penniless and homeless. He stretched out on the king size bed and switched the television on to watch some daytime programmes as boring as they were, it would take him away from his situation until he had to check out at 2pm, then it wouldn't be long before Carol finished work.

Carol spent her shift running around here there and everywhere, but it didn't stop her thinking about seeing Ben later. She had made up her mind that IF she could help him she would, but she wouldn't put herself, her son or her job at risk for him though. If there was a chance where drugs were left lying around or the drugs cabinet left open with no-one around, then she would possibly take some, if there was no risk of getting caught.

Finally, Jason had said that that was enough for today and to go home. Carol realized she hadn't had chance to text Ben again. She pulled her phone out of here pocket and quickly sent a Ben a text saying she was sorry for not texting earlier and that she was just finishing and if he wanted to pick her up she would wait in the hospital café for him. Ben instantly replied he would be there within 15 minutes and that he couldn't wait to see her. This brought a smile to

Carols face, she got changed into her own clothes and made sure her makeup was as perfect as she could make it and made her way to the Café and sat down with a takeaway cup of coffee and one for Ben.

Carol spotted his car sat at the lights waiting to come into the hospital, so she went outside and waited at the roadside for him.

Carol gave him a big smile as he pulled up alongside her, she opened the door and got in, leaning across to give him a kiss, as she leant back, she noticed all the bags on the back seat, "What's that all about?" she asked, "Don't worry about that, I will tell you about that later, at the moment I'm just so pleased to see you again." "And I'm pleased to see you too," Carol said leaning across and kissing Ben on his cheek, just as the cars behind started blasting on their horns, as Ben was holding up all the traffic behind him, bringing his window down, he waved to the car behind and drove away. "Well that's a good start," said Carol, "what do you mean?" Ben asked, "Well before you would have had let rip at that driver and give him the finger as you drove away, but this time you just waved, and all is happy with the world." "Hey even I can change" Ben said smiling, "let's hope so," came the reply.

As they drove to Carols house, they laughed and joked about each other and declaring how much they had missed each other. When they pulled up outside her house, Ben jumped out and ran around the car and opened her door, "why what a gentleman," she quipped. "Nothing but the best for my fine lady, by the way you are my fine lady?" he asked. "Ask me that again in the morning and I will give you an answer." Carol laughed.

29

The next morning after a very passionate night, Carol and Ben were sat having breakfast, "Carol hun, I have a very big favour to ask, you can say no but I hope you don't, last night you asked me about the bags in the back of my car. The reason for this is that my bank account was hacked a few months ago, and now the bank is insisting that it was my debit card that was used and refuse to pay any of my direct debits and because of this my landlord kicked me out, my phone is due to be cut off any day now and the bank don't get a damn that they have left me with just £10 to my name. My question is can you put me up for a little while until I manged to get things sorted?" "Wow that came out of the blue, I will need some time to think about it as it is a massive step, you can stay here while I'm at work today and we will talk about it tonight." "Thank you hun and it goes without saying I will take you to and from work and anywhere else you need to go."

In his head Ben was shouting YES.

Carol arrived at the hospital full of the joy of spring, "Somebody must have got some last night," Jason said as Carol passed him by, "What in the earth do mean Jason?"

"Oh, come on. Just look at your face, you have a smile so big a Cheshire cat would be proud of it," Carol's face went bright red and she murmured, "sod off Jason."

As they walked into the A&E department, they were met with a department that was rammed with patients and the staff struggling to cope. "It's time for us to roll up our sleeves and dive on in there, Carol" "Can't we just hide in a corner," Carol laughed. "Get your backside into Resus and do what you do best and make people better." Jason said putting his arm around Carols shoulders.

It was a little quieter in Resus, only 2 of the 6 beds were occupied, the first bed had a patient with chest pains, and the second was a motorcyclist who had had an argument with a bollard and came worse off. Both patients were in a comfortable position and not needing Carol's help. She went about restocking the Resus room. Just as she was finishing this task the red phone chirped away. Picking up the phone Carol said, "Swindon Resus," "Good morning Resus, this is Dean on unit 27, we are bringing you in a 30 something female who has overdosed on prescription medication.

She is GCS10 B/P 79/54 resp 9 we are concerned she will crash at anytime, we will be with you in 8 minutes." "Okay we will be ready." Carol said hanging up the receiver. Picking up the microphone she announced, "Urgent medical call 8 minutes." Carol then went into bay 3 and began to prepare it for the patient, making sure there was an ECG and Defib machine ready, she asked the doctor who had just arrived what medication he wanted ready.

We better have some Naloxone and Adrenaline and Prochlorperazine anti sickness. Carol went and got the keys for the cabinet from Jason who was still in Majors. "How's it going in there?" Jason asked. "We are expecting an O/D, but apart from that it's not too bad, I am just getting the drugs ready for the incoming patient." Jason handed over the keys and Carol made her way to the cabinet, when she opened it her thoughts turned to Ben, making sure no-one was watching she removed a strip on Morphine tablets and put them in her pocket.

Selecting the other drug's, she needed she took the keys back to Jason saying "Did you know that the drugs cabinet was unlocked? Whoever opened it last could not have locked it properly."

"It was one of the consultants," Jason replied, "I will have a word with him later, thanks for letting me know." With that Carol returned to the Resus room.

At lunchtime Carol texted Ben to see how he was doing, he replied by saying that he had washed up and hoovered the downstairs, aww bless him she thought, it will be a nice surprise for him when I give him the pills.

The rest of Carols shift was mundane to say the least, so much so, for the last 2 hours of her shift she worked alongside Jason helping in Majors.

Carol finished her shift at 3.30pm and was pleased that Ben was there to meet her as it meant she didn't have to take the bus and spend the next 45 minutes stuck next to god knows who.

A similar pattern occurred over the next several weeks, sometimes she managed to get Ben some pills sometimes she couldn't. On the days that she couldn't she could see the disappointment in Ben's face and one day he even got a little angry about it but that soon disappeared with a hug and a kiss. But at no time did she feel pressurised in doing it. Until one day at work, a Policeman stopped her in a hallway, in a very nasty manner he informed her that he knew that she used to get Ben drugs out of the hospital and now it was time for her to get some for him or he would report what he knew to the senior staff and she would end up losing her job and more than likely be prosecuted as well. He demanded her phone number and said he would call her in the next couple of days. This shook Carol too her core and phoned Ben straight away, "Hello hun, I wasn't expecting you to ring," he said. "Ben, I have a massive problem, can you come to the hospital in my lunchbreak?" "Why what's up babe?" Bens brain was going faster than it had ever had. "I can't talk now, I will text you a time later, but Ben please turn up, I really need to talk to you urgently, I have to go now as we are busy in Resus, but Ben please turn up." He promised he would and she then hung up the phone and nervously return to Resus.

After Carol had hung up, Ben just stood there wondering what the hell could have happened for Carol to be in such a panic that she wanted to meet him as soon as possible. He did consider packing his stuff and running away but he had nowhere to go and nobody knew he was here and to be honest he really liked her, so he decided to meet up with her and find out what was going on and then if it needed he would take off before she finished her shift.

Two and a half long hours later, Carol text and said to meet in the canteen in 30 minutes. Ben arrived just as Carol was pacing outside the entrance, "Let's go and sit in your car," she said, "I don't want anyone over hearing what I have to say." This worried Ben even more. Once sat in the car, Ben held onto her hands and said, "Okay deep breath, tell me what is going on."

At that point Carol burst into tears and though the sobbing she told Ben all about what had happened and how she was scared of the Policeman and that she didn't want to lose her job. To himself Ben thought 'Fuck', but to Carol he said let me think about this for a second. "Right!" Ben said, "did he say anything about me and where I was?" "No" Carol sobbed, it was then Ben realised it was '30' who had stopped Carol. "Good then if you trust me, I will sort it, right at this moment I don't know how, but by time you have finished your shift I will have sorted it. He won't report you as he needs you more then you need him to keep quiet, so even if he does phone you, just say you are not a work for a few days but would be back on shift on whatever day comes to mind." Ben reached across and took her in his arms and whispered, "I promise I will make it right." "Do you really promise to make right Ben?" "I promise" he said believing the words that he had said. "Come on dry your eyes, let's go and get a coffee and something to eat, I think you need it." Carol took a big sniff, pulled a hanky out of her bag, wiped away the tears and blew her nose.

She then pulled down the sun visor and said, "Look at the state of me, how could you fancy such an ugly troll," in a half serious note. "My darling you are an angel not a troll and any man with a penis would fancy the pants off you, even the gay ones." This made her chuckle, "oh Ben, I am still very worried about it though." "Don't you worry, I said I would get it sorted and for you I will make sure I get it sorted. Now come on I am thirsty, and a cup of hospital coffee is just what the doctor didn't order."

30

After leaving the hospital, Ben drove back to Carol's place, sitting in the kitchen with a coffee, Ben contemplated what steps he could do about DS Jones, he knew he had to report the copper, but how to and to who. He could phone crimestoppers but that would take too long, he could phone the Serious Crime Squad, but with his recent run in with them that was out of the question, he could phone Police internal investigations, but once again that would take too long. Ben decided what he would do was to write down everything he could remember about his dealings with the DS and contact the Detective Chief Inspector of the drugs squad direct and tell him everything, leaving out anything that could get himself arrested.

An hour later Ben had written over 5 pages of places, times etc. of things he could remember. Before making the call, Ben decided he need a spliff to calm his nerves. So as not to stink the house out, he went for a walk around the block, by time he got back he was resolute in what he was doing, because he realised just how much Carol meant to him and he wanted to protect her anyway he could.

"Swindon Police, how can I help you," the voice said, "Can I speak to the DCI of the drugs squad and it's only him or her I want to speak too, also can you tell me their name please." "It's is Alan Munro, and I will try and put you through now, but it may go through to his voicemail." The phone went silent for a few seconds, then a booming voice said "Munro" "Mr Munro, I don't want to give my name, but I need to talk to you urgently about one of your officers," The DCI glanced at his caller id and wrote down the number displayed on his blotter, as Ben had forgotten to put 141 before dialling the number, "I'm listening," the DCI said. Ben went onto explain all the details of his complaint to the DCI, when he had finished the DCI said "This is a very serious matter son, before I take it any further, this is not just a gripe you have with my officer because he arrested you for having some weed on you is it? And that's the reason you won't give your name!" "No sir, every word I have said to you is the complete truth and I hope you believe me, as he has threatened another friend of mine, who is a female and very frightened and he can't be allowed to continue his reign of terror." The DCI said that he always takes complaints very seriously and it will be investigated thoroughly.

Ben thanked the DCI and hung up the phone with a very shaky hand. Oh My God, what have I done, Ben thought to himself, have I opened a can of worms that is going to come back and bite me so hard, that there will be no way out for me in the end. With a resigned shrug Ben thought it was too late now, then he threw up in the sink.

DCI Munroe sat there strumming his fingers on his desk, he had heard through the gripe vine that Jones had gone a little rogue, but this was more than a little rogue.

He really was a good DS, but he would not have a totally corrupt officer on his squad. He picked up his phone and called The Independent Police Complaints Commission (IPCC). "Good Afternoon this is DCI Munroe at Swindon, I have received a genuine complaint about one of my DS's and I want your advice on what my next steps should be."

"What and how serious is the complaint?" the person from the IPCC asked. After explaining about the phone call and the contents of the complaint the IPCC recommended the instant suspension of the officer concerned, and that the file was handed over to them to investigate it independently. The DCI reluctantly agreed to this course of action and said he would call Jones in straight away and put him on suspension and he would also make his own enquiries and inform them of his results and asked for the IPCC to keep him informed of their enquiries. Before ending the call, the DCI gave the person from the IPCC the phone number that the caller had used.

DCI Munro walked out of his office and into the squad room, "Where is DS Jones?" he demanded to know, "I'm not sure," said a DC, "Find him and tell to get in my office asap like yesterday." The DCI said as he went back to his office, slamming the door behind. "Holy shit, the DS seems to have pissed off the DCI big time," The DC said to his colleague. "Any idea where the DS could be?" "I think he is out and about, I will ring him, if he answers that is another matter."

It took 15 minutes of constantly trying the DS's number before he answered it, "What the fuck do you want?" the DS grumbled, "Boss the DCI wants you in his office straight away and just to give you a heads up he is in one hell of a mood, the whole building shook when he slammed his door shut."

"I wonder what has bit his fucking arse?" Jones said to himself, well he can fucking wait for me, I'm not running back at his fucking command." "I will be there as soon as I can," he said to the DC. What the DS did not realize was the longer he kept the DCI waiting, the angrier the DCI became. After an hour the DCI stormed into the squad room again, and with his booming voice, so as everyone could hear he said, "Where the fuck is DS Jones?" "I spoke to him a short while ago and he said he would be right in." One of the DC's said. "How long ago was a short while ago?" the DCI demanded. Just then DS Jones walked into the squad room, "My office, NOW!" The DCI boomed, pointing at the DS.

"Sit," the DCI told DS Jones, "David you are in some sort of shit situation, today I received a formal complaint against you, which has gone to the IPCC and from that, internal affairs will want to question you, I have heard the rumor's going around the station, but up to now I have ignored them because of your outstanding work in the squad, but now it is official I have no option but to suspend you with immediate effect and warn you about interfering with any potential witnesses.

Also, you are not allowed to have any contact with any serving officer or civilian worker attached to this station." As the DCI shifted some paperwork on his desk, Jones spotted a number on his blotter and thought he recognized it, so he remembered the last four digits, hoping not only was the number in his contact list but it would also tell him who had possibly grassed him up. "With all that in mind I'm going to ask you to hand in your warrant card and to leave the station straight away and not talking to anyone on your way out, I will of course be informing the squad of the situation and reminding them that while the case is active they will not be allowed to have any contact with you either on a professional or friendly basis. Also, if they do, that they will be suspended and investigated as well. I will not expect you to make any comment at this time as it may very well prejudice your case."

The DS stood up reached into his wallet and handed over his warrant card and left the building without saying a word out loud to anyone.

Once outside he brought up his list of contacts and started going through the numbers, it didn't take him very long to discover it was one of the numbers Ben Thorton had used in the past. Thinking to himself, he thought if you have grassed me up Benny boy and if I find you, you are a very much dead Benny boy.

31

Just to make Carol even more pissed off, as she was wanting to get home to see if Ben had managed to sort things out. Jason had somehow talked her into doing a double shift. Sister Joan was short staffed for the night shift and using the fact that Carol had just comeback off leave. He said it in such a way she couldn't refuse. "Jason you are a complete swine," she said, "using the 'leave' card and that Sister and I work well together, but if you let me have first dibs on the off-duty rota then I will do it, but I do need to have something to eat and let my mum and Ben know I won't be home tonight." "Okay, once you are clear in Resus, disappear for 45 minutes, I will let Joan know that you will be in the staff café if she needs you urgently.

Once she was in the café, she called her mum first, as that would be the quickest call, then she called Ben. "Ben, I am really sorry, but I now have to work a double shift and won't be home tonight, you are more than welcome to stay there, if we are quiet,

I will call you for a chat to keep you company. By the way have you sorted out the other problem?" "Yes, I have started to sort it, but it will take a little while," "What do you mean a little while? Ben, he threatened to tell my bosses, I haven't got a little while." "What I have done is to report him to his big boss and he is going to investigate him. I reckon while he is being investigated he will be suspended, so he won't be able to use his Police powers, so you will be okay." "Do you really think it will be okay darling." A smile spread across Bens face as that was the first time she had called him 'darling'. Ben thought he would try his luck with the romantic stuff. "Sweetheart, I am sure as I can be." Just like Ben, Carol smiled, and her heart skipped a beat at the sound of 'sweetheart'.

Unfortunately, for them both Carol had had the night from hell, with the stabbing and MI, but it had given Carol the chance to get some Diamorphine which was now in her bra.

At just before 8am Carol text Ben saying she would be finishing in 15 minutes and would he be so kind and come and pick her up, as she had a little present for him, he texted back saying he had a big present for her, putting a big LOL at the end of the message.

Ben was standing outside of his car, when Carol walked out, "Wow what a sight for tired eyes," Ben said as he pulled her close to him, kissing her deeply, holding onto her tightly, he whispered "Carol I love you with all my heart." "I love you too, now about my 'Big' surprise, do I get it before or after breakfast she giggled. "How about instead of?" "Yeah sounds good to me. When they arrived home, Ben made the coffee while Carol took off her uniform, standing there in her undies. Carol reached inside her bra and brought out the vials of Diamorphine and put them on the kitchen worktop. Ben picked one up and looked at it, "Baby, I have been thinking about you and drugs all night and I never want you to bring anymore drugs home ever, you mean far too much to me. It's about time I cleaned up my act and led an honest life with a proper job and be there for you and little Josh and maybe even one day do the marriage thing. But I will sell these, holding up the vials of Diamorphine, just to give us a little money to start a nest egg for the future." "Ben do you really mean all what you just said or are you just playing with me to get into my knickers?" "Yes, I mean every word, I have never thought I would ever settle down, but you make me want to be in a relationship and yes I want to get into your knickers." Carol couldn't have been happier if someone had told her she had won the triple rollover lottery.

A few days later, Ben received a text he was half expecting but was hoping that it would take quite a while before it did arrive. It read, I know it was you who grassed me up, and for that you are going to pay the ultimate price. Ben was really shaken up by the last line, he didn't know how Jones had worked out it was him, but it was too late to change things now. Ben wondered how he could forward this message to DCI, without revealing his identity. In the end he decided he would ring the DCI, explain what the message had said and ask if the DCI had a mobile number he could forward the text to him. Not only that it would give a number he could use in an emergency.

"Munro" the booming voice said, "Good morning Mr Munro, I rang you about DS Jones, somehow and I don't know how, but he managed to obtain my number and has sent me a death threat by text. Have you got a mobile number so as I can forward it to you, also have you any idea how he got my number?" "Allow me to say, I have no idea how he got your number and I can reassure you that I will pass any information you give me on to the Police Complaints Commission, and yes I will give you my personal number. It really would help us if we knew who you are, so as we could protect you if necessary." Ben thought about that for a few seconds and replied "At the moment I would rather not divulge my name, but If the threats keep coming, I may change my mind, but only to protect my girlfriend who has nothing to do with this.

After finishing the call, Munro thought how Jones got the number. The answer became clear as he moved his newspaper off his blotter, there in full view was the phone number of the informant. Jones must either have known the number or memorised it. Bollocks, how could he have made such a stupid mistake.

The message tone on his mobile brought him back into the room. Opening it, it was just as the young man had said, it didn't say he would be killed but it truly implied it. He called his contact at IPCC and passed on the text.

32

"Who were talking too?" Carol asked, "The Chief Inspector of the drugs squad, I was just giving him more information on that copper Jones," "Does this mean he will be arrested?" "No idea, but I really hope so, I just want to give them as much as I can remember to make the case stronger, everything I have told them is the gospel truth." "Good. I have to go over to my mums as I haven't seen Josh for 2 days now, he will start to think I have left him, do you want to come with me?" "Do you think your mum will mind?" "I don't care, you are part of my life now and I want the both of you to get on, she knows nothing about the drugs and I want to keep it way, so if mum asks what you do for a living, please don't say drug dealer." Carol laughed. "How about the King of England in waiting?" "If only you were that good looking" she quipped back. "What shift are you on today hun?" "3.30pm to 10.30pm." "How about when you have finished, we go and get a kebab?"

"If you can wait that before eating I think that's a great idea." "Done deal."

When Carol arrived for work later that afternoon, Lizzie was in the changing rooms, "Afternoon hun, Carol said, "I am glad you didn't say 'good afternoon'" "why is that?" "Just having a shitty day, me and Trevor had a major barney. I am sure he is cheating on me, I can't prove it, let's just say it's a gut feeling but something just isn't right, he hasn't been near me for ages, he must be getting it somewhere." "Maybe it's your shift pattern, it isn't conducive to a romantic relationship if you are not careful." As they walked out of the changing rooms, their attention was directed to the drugs cabinet, standing there was Matron, Jason, Sister Joan and the student nurse Joanne, plus 2 other men in suits. "What the hell is going on over there," Lizzie asked a passing nurse, "Something about drugs missing, and the student nurse isn't really a nurse, she is an undercover Police woman."

Carol went white as a ghost, her legs were turning into jelly, her brain desperately trying to take in everything that was being said, but all she could think of was that bent copper, had he kept his word and told on her?

"You alright Carol?" "Yeah stomach cramps, time of the month, give me a minute just going to run to the loo."

After checking there was no-one else in the toilet, she Locked herself in the cubicle, she grabbed her phone and phoned Ben. "Ben what the fuck am I going to do, there are police officers here, because they have discovered there are drugs missing, not only that, Joanne the student nurse is actually an undercover policewoman, what if she has been watching me Ben, I could go to prison." "Ben" she cried, "I don't know what to do." "Honey take a deep breath, I know this is easier to say, then do, but please don't panic, you need to brave this out, you need to find out what exactly is going, not just hearsay.

Where are you now?" "Hiding in the toilets." Well that is a sign of a guilty person, you need to go out like nothing's wrong and find out for yourself, is your boss Jason around?" "Yes, he is with the rest of them stood by the drugs cabinet, ok what about lizzie is she working today?" "Yeah she was with me when we noticed what was going on." "Good, make your face up, and go and find her and see if she knows what is going on." "Oh, Ben I am so scared, what if it is me they are after." "If it is you then you tell them that I had threatened you that if you do as I said I would hurt Josh. There is no way I will let you take any blame for this, with my dealings with the Police,

they will believe you that I did that. I will be here waiting for the police; just tell them I am forcing you to let me stay here and leave the rest to me. Or you can call me if it's not you they are after." "Ben, I love you so much, I know your past is shady but it's now I worry about, and I never want to lose you."

"And I love you so much too, and hopefully are lives together will be long and extremely happy. Now go and find out what is what."

Carol made her way back out into A&E, Lizzie was in the same place as she had left her, "Feeling better hun?" "Yeah thanks, so what is happening?" "You are not going to believe it, but you know Dr Anderson from plastic's." "Yeah," Well he has been caught stealing morphine and other drugs, apparently, he is addicted to them, Sister Joan had noticed the drugs were being stolen. Along with Matron and NHS Fraud, they set up a sting operation using Joanne as their eyes and ears. She noticed that he was going to the cabinet to take drugs and instead of returning unused drugs he was keeping them." "OMG a few weeks ago I was called into Matrons office and questioned about some drugs that Dr Anderson took off me, saying he would return them, but he didn't, and he told Jason that I didn't give them to him." "My god you were lucky then."

"My stomach is hurting, excuse me for a minute." Carol went back to the toilet and phoned Ben, as soon as he answered she said, "It wasn't me Ben it wasn't me," "What was it all about then?" "One of the doctors is addicted to pain killers and they had set a trap up for him, oh Ben I was so scared, I don't think I ever could do it again, I know you said you wouldn't ever ask me again but if you did, I wouldn't do it." "I promised you I never would, and I will keep that promise to you for the rest of my life. You can relax now and enjoy your shift and when your finished I will treat you to that kebab cos I know how to treat a woman right." She laughed. "Thank you for being there for me darling, I can't wait to give you a big thank you kiss." "Can I choose where the kiss is planted," he said cheekily. "Of course, the kiss will go wherever you say," "My lips sound like a good place to me."

"Oh, you are boring!" Carol said with a pretend huffiness in her voice. "See you later, love you," "I love you to Carol with all my heart."

Carol's shift was a very rare shift; they didn't have a single red phone call for the whole shift. Before she knew it, the shift was over, and Ben was waiting right outside the entrance as promised. They made their way to the nearest mobile kebab shop. While they were waiting to be served a car pulled up and two occupants got out and walked over to the serving counter, one of the men looked across and said, "Alright Ben," "Oh shit" Ben thought, it was only one of 30's informers, now it would only be a short while before 30 knew where he was living. Ben moved closer to Carol and whispered, "we may have a problem this guy is one of DS Jones informers, when we leave here I will be driving very fast, I don't want them knowing where you live,

228

Go and get into the car without showing your face if at all possible. Carol did what was asked of her, making sure her seatbelt was on tightly. "Hi Ben, you not talking to us anymore? Just because 30 is looking everywhere for you and he is offering a grand to anyone who gets an address for you." Picking up his food, he turned to the man and said, "Go fuck yourself and tell 30 to fuck himself too."

Ben ran to his car, started it up and pulled out of the car park spinning all four wheels, turning right Carol said, "we are going the wrong way to my place." "We are not going to go directly to yours, if you look in the mirror, you'll see a car which is now following us and probably on the phone to Jones at the same time, don't worry I will lose them soon, I know the driver and he is crap at driving, just hope Jones is not in the area, as that would be a whole new problem, so hold on tight it's time to get rid of our tail.

Twisting and turning around corners speeding up to 80mph in a 30 zone, it took Ben about 5 minutes to lose the person following him, he quickly made his way to Carol's fearful that every set of headlights in his rear-view mirror might be DS Jones. Ben dropped Carol off outside her house saying he was going to park the car the car a couple streets away. When got back to the house instead of finding Carols in tears she was exactly the opposite she was hyped up saying "that was fantastic I never driven that fast or dangerously before, can't wait to do it again." "Let's hope we never have to do that again," was the reply.

33

DS Jones was so pissed off, that little fucking weasel had escaped his clutches by the skin of his teeth, if only he hadn't been having sex with one of his contacts, he would have Ben Thorton right where he wanted him, under his boot, getting the kicking that he deserved.

Well it answered the question that Thorton was still in Swindon, probably with that tart nurse. All of a sudden, a light bulb switched on his brain. You idiot, David, you don't have to search all over Swindon for him, all you have to do is put a watch on the hospital, then Ben would serve himself to you on a plate. All he needed was Ben's car registration number and bingo, game over for the little shit.

Jones called Stuart Williamson, "Hi Stuart it's 30," "Any news of Ben's whereabouts?" Stuart asked. "No not yet, but do you have his car's registration number?"

"No, I haven't" "Shit, I could do with it," "hold on a sec, I will call you right back." Stuart said.

A few minutes later, Stuart rang 30, "Sorry about that, but I remembered that I had a picture of his car on my computer, and guess what, it shows his registration plate." After giving the number to 30, he said "I owe you big time Stuart, and soon as I am done with him, I will let you know where the little shit is, so as you can go and batter him some more." "I'll look forward to that call 30."

After getting off the phone with Stuart, thought about it seriously, he couldn't risk the chance of being seen handing out the punishment or even being anywhere nearby. Thinking about it he thought, I will get a couple of 'Yardies' to come down from the smoke and sort out this little problem. It will cost him more than the grand he was offering, but he could be certain they would do a proper job on Ben.

Two days later, Ben didn't notice the black and grey Audi, with the heavily tinted windows on the front row of the hospital car park as he dropped Carol off for work, he also didn't notice the window of the black and grey Audi being lowered and a picture being taken of both him and Carol as they got out to hug goodbye, and Ben wasn't to know that the passenger of the black and grey Audi was now sending that picture of them to DS Jones to get conformation that they had the right person, he also wasn't aware that DS Jones had texted back and said yes that was him and to go ahead but to leave the girl alone, as he wanted to deal with her personally.

Ben also didn't notice that the black and grey Audi had fallen in 3 cars behind him as he left the car park. The driver of the Audi was careful not to show out, even when Ben stopped in the garage for fuel or even when he went into a large supermarket to do a little shopping, the passenger just got out of the car and followed Ben on foot.

When Ben got back to his car, the placed the shopping on the back seat and drove out of the supermarket car park with ELO's 'Mr Blue Skies blasting out at top volume, today is going to be a good day, he thought to himself, finally I'm getting my life on track.

As had become the custom for Ben he parked his car a few streets away from Carols and started to walk to the house, this was the first time he noticed the black and grey Audi with heavily tinted windows.

Instantly he realised he had seen the car in the supermarket car park but only subconsciously. The hair on the back of his neck stood up, as the two occupants jumped out of the car. Ben dropped his shopping to the floor and started to run, the two men were faster and fitter then him and they caught up with him before Ben had reached the corner of the road. "This is for 30," one of them said just before landing a blow to the side of Bens head that sent him to the floor.

The kicks came raining in as Ben desperately tried to get to his feet to try and fight them off. As he got to his knees a kick caught him in his stomach, taking the wind out of him and sending him back onto the floor. Somehow from somewhere deep inside of him, Ben managed to find the strength to stand up despite the punches and kicks and start landing punches and kicks of his own, soon it was one on one as one of the attackers had disappeared. Ben was amazed at his own determination and fight.

Ben didn't see the second attacker return from behind him, he just heard the swoosh noise, as Ben turned his head, the machete made contact with Ben's neck. Ben hit the floor and his eyes closed, he didn't even feel the final kicks to his prostrate body.

Bens attackers ran back to their car and drove off. A neighbour who had heard the commotion had made a note of the cars make and number, while on the phone to the Police the neighbour just walked towards the figure laying in a heap in the middle of the road not realizing how bad the victim was hurt, as he got closer the neighbours face went white, panicking he shouted down the phone OMG they've nearly chopped his head off.

34

There were very few people in the Resus room when the red phone went off. "Good morning Swindon Resus," Carol said. "This is a red alert call, we are bringing you a male mid to late 20's with a partial decapitation, we can't get any readings at all, but he is still breathing, we will be with you in approx. 7 minutes." Hanging up, Carol couldn't believe what she was hearing. Pulling herself together, she switched on the microphone and said, "This is a red alert call, I repeat a red alert call, can we have a trauma, a medical, a plastics and a cardiac team to Resus I repeat, this is a red alert call, trauma medical plastics and cardiac teams to Resus immediately."

Jason came running through the Resus doors closely followed members of the different teams. "What is the call?" Jason asked Carol. "A partial decapitation, male mid to late 20's no readings but breathing, "WHAT? How the hell is he still breathing?"

Carol just shrugged her shoulders. "Anyone else I need to call?" "A vicar maybe." Jason said half joking half serious.

Going from very few people in Resus, it was now nearly full with medic's, the noise level was going through the roof. "QUIET!" Jason shouted at the top of his voice, just and the lead consultant of the A&E Dept came into Resus. "What have we got Jason?" she asked. Jason explained the call. "Right listen up, I want an anaesthetist and plastics at the patient's head, I want trauma beside the patient cut side and I want cardiac the other side of the patient, anyone else please stand back and wait to be called forward. Jason, I want you on notes, and Carol I want you on an open line to the blood bank. How long before the patient arrives?" "It was 7 minutes," Carol said, "but that was 4 minutes ago." "Okay I want every door between here and the ambulance bay open and manned, I don't want to see any patients or relatives or anyone else between there and here."

"Here it comes." Someone said.

The paramedics brought Ben into the Resus room. Carol let out an ear-piercing scream. "What the fuck?" the consultant said, "That's Ben, that's my boyfriend, with that Carol passed out. "Get her out of here and make sure you look after her." The consultant said to one of the medic's. "Right let's get to work." She continued.

As hard as they tried, the medical teams couldn't get Ben to maintain any blood pressure, his heart rate dropped to less than 10 beats a minute, then it stopped altogether, they managed to restart his heart, but it would only last for a minute or two then stop again. "We are not going to win this one, I'm afraid. The lead consultant stated. "Keep pumping the fluids and let autopulse continue, I am going to talk to Carol."

She found Carol in the relative's room, with a group of nurses around her, Carol was sobbing her heart out. "She sat down beside her, put her arm around her and said,

"I know this is a stupid question, but how are you doing?" "Shit how is Ben doing?" "I am really sorry Carol, but we are losing the battle, and to be honest, his body just can't take anymore, do you feel strong enough to come in and say goodbye before he goes?" This made Carol cry even harder, but she said she would come in. Being held up by 2 nurses, Carol entered Resus, which fell silent when she came in. Sobbing loudly, she made her way to the head of the bed, as she bent down and kissed him, Ben's heart stopped again. One of the medics went to move in and the consultant waved him away, shaking her head.

Carol throw her arms over Ben's body and sobbed uncontrollably. In a quiet voice the Consultant announced "Time of death 10.37am. She then ushered most of the teams out of the cubicle. Jason walked over to Carol, with tears falling down his face, he held her and said, "I'm so sorry hun." Carol responded with "Why did he have to kill him, why?" Jason thought he must have misheard, but didn't want to upset Carol even more, so he decided to remember what she said, so he could clear it up later as it sounded really important, as it indicated Carol knew who had killed Ben. The consultant had also heard what Carol had said. She didn't know if the Police would want Carol with the body, so she said to her that they had to complete what they needed to do and that she could come back in later.

Jason and Lizzie led Carol back to the waiting room, "Keep an eye on her," Jason said. He went back into the Resus room, and took the consultant to one side, did you hear what I thought I heard?" "Yes I did. I think we better talk to the Police before we can allow Carol back in there." "I agree, I will get onto them now and direct them your way as well."

35

Detective Keith Gregory, arrived at the hospital in the pouring rain, around 30 minutes after Ben had died. The receptionist took him through to the doctors and nurses station and introduced him to Jason who in turn introduced him to Emma Thruxton who was the lead A&E consultant on duty today. "Can you tell me the events of this morning please?" he asked. The three of them went into the consultant's office and closed the door behind them.

Emma started by saying, "We received a red alert call, which is our highest call, meaning the chance of immediate death or life changing symptoms at 09.11, informing us that a paramedic team was bringing us a patient who was partially decapitated but breathing. On reaching our Resus room, it was then that one of our Resus nurses discovered to her horror that it was her boyfriend. Despite all our efforts I pronounced him dead at 10.27am."

"Oh my god, that poor nurse," DS Gregory said, "So we have a positive identification then?" He continued.

"Yes" Jason said, "His name was Ben Thorton." The look of surprise was clearly written all over DS Gregory's face. "By the look on your face you know Ben then?" Jason asked. "Well I didn't know him personally, but I was investigating him in to the death of his previous partner Tina Williamson. Did he manage to say anything at all before he died?" "No" Emma said, "But Carol Mcvitie, his girlfriend did say, and I quote "Why did he have to kill him?" we both heard him," Emma said pointing towards Jason, "That's correct, but one thing, are you sure it's the same person? As I have had long conversations with Carol about her relationship with Ben and she never ever mentioned that Ben was being questioned about a murder let alone the murder of his ex-partner." "As far as I know it is one and the same Ben Thorton. Is Carol still here?" "Yes" Jason said, "she is in my office."

"I need to talk to her urgently to find out who 'HE' is. Can you take me to her please?" "Of course, Emma are you going to come with us?" "No, I will let you take it from here, but call me straight away if you need me." "Will do."

Jason and DS Gregory entered Jason's office and found Carol still sobbing along with Lizzie, who was holding Carol and sobbing. "Carol, this is DS Keith Gregory of Swindon Police and he needs to ask you some questions." Gregory could see a look of sheer panic come across Carol's face. "Carol, I know there is never a good time, but I need to ask you a couple of question's now." Carol sobbed okay. "Carol when Ben died, the staff heard you say why did he have to kill him, do you remember saying that?" Carol just nodded her head. "Can I ask who he is and why he would want to kill Ben?" Carol looked at Jason then at Lizzie then at the floor and finally at him. Stumbling with her words and with the sobs it was hard for the DS to understand what she was saying. "I'm sorry Carol, but I need to understand what you are saying, do you think you could take a deep breath and start again?" Carol blew her nose, wiped her eyes and tried to stop sobbing, "I said, he is a Police officer the name of Jones, but everyone knows him as 30 and that Ben had reported him to his big boss for threatening to kill Ben." Do you know if Jones is a normal copper or does he work for a specialist department?" "He works for the department that deals with drugs. It must be DS David Jones, Gregory thought to himself, if this is right, Gregory knew he was well over his head and needed his DI here now, but his DI and DCI were in a meeting with the Assistant Chief Constable. Gregory knew he had to interrupt the meeting. Then it struck him, if it was Jones then Carol needed protecting urgently in case he went after her as well.

"Thank you, Carol, I know it was hard and the last thing you needed right now, but we can now focus our investigation in the right direction. I need to contact my boss, who will with no doubt come and ask you exactly the same questions, I am sorry about it, but it is the way we have to do things, so we get things right the first time." Once again Carol just nodded. As the DS got up to leave he said, "Oh Carol, did you and Ben have any children?" "No, why? I have my own little boy Josh; why do you need to know that?" It's so we can satisfy that everyone is safe and well and stay that way. Where is Josh? At school?" "No, he is with my mum, you don't think he will go after my little boy, do you?" Carol said getting hysterical. "I don't think so, but to help settle your mind, if you give me her address I will send a car around there and pick them up and take them somewhere safe, if you want." "Yes, yes please." She answered through the tears and gave the DS her mums address.

DS Gregory went outside and thought about calling SO19, but the thought of two burly coppers all dressed in black carrying machine guns, scaring the hell out of an old lady and young child, didn't sit well with him, so instead he called the SCU office.

"SCU, Heather Smithson," "Heather it's Keith, I'm working on this murder case and I need you and Jenny to draw weapons and go to the following address and pick up a grandmother and grandchild and take them to a place of safety, do not use your comm's only use you own mobile phones, as this may involve a serving Police Officer." "Okay Keith, I will call you as soon as we have picked them up."

After drawing their pistols from the armoury, Heather and Jenny made their way to the address in East Swindon. The door was opened by a typical looking grandmother, "Mrs Mcvitie?" "Yes, how can I help you?" Showing Mrs Mcvitie her Police Identification "My name is Heather Smithson and I am from Swindon Police, and this is my colleague Jenny Parker, can we come in please?" The blood drained from Mrs Mcvitie's face, "What's is going on? Has something happened to Carol?" Jenny put her arm around her and guided her into her front room, where they found Josh playing with his toy dinosaurs. He looked up, smiled and said "Hello." "Hello Josh," Heather said, "I like your Dinosaur's, can I sit and play with them with you?" Josh nodded his head, so Heather sat on the floor with him while Jenny started speaking to the grandmother. "There has been an incident in which Carol is indirectly involved. Do you know her boyfriend?" "Yes, it's Ben, why?" "I'm afraid to say Ben has died in circumstances which may affect Carol, so as a precaution she is being looked after at the hospital and she has asked us to pick you and Josh up and take you somewhere safe." "Is Carol safe and well?" "Yes, she is being well looked after, if you can get an overnight bag together for both you and Josh, we will meet up with your daughter later."

36

As Gregory made his way back to his car, he tried to ring his DI, but the call went straight to answerphone, so he tried the DCI, but that also went to answerphone. He called the comm's room and asked to be put through to the ACC offices and not to be told no, as this was very urgent. The ACC answered his phone after just a few rings, "Good Morning sir, this is DS Gregory and I need to speak to my DI urgently, as we have a murder case which may involve a serving Police Officer. The ACC handed the phone over to the DI saying, "I think you better take this; it is DS Gregory." "This better be very urgent or you will regret it." The DI said. "Well I believe if there is a murder where a serving Police Officer maybe involved, it would be classed as urgent Sir." "I'm listening." "Sir, do you remember I was working on the Tina Williamson case and the name Ben Thorton came up?" "Yes, why?" "Well he was murdered this morning and here is the kicker, his girlfriend say's it was Detective Sergeant David Jones of the drug squad."

"Whoa, backup, I thought Thorton murdered his girlfriend, how the hell did she get the information to you, via a medium?"

"No sir that was his ex-girlfriend who died, this is his new girlfriend, who by the way is a nurse and was working in A&E when Ben Thorton was brought in with his head virtually chopped off. She saw what had happened to him and as you may expect she is totally devastated." "Okay but how is DS Jones involved" "As I said she said that she believes DS Jones killed Ben or had him killed as the DS has been threatening them and she also claims that the DS is as bent as they come. So, bent in fact, she said Ben Thorton had reported Jones to his DCI and he is now being investigated." "How much credence are you putting on what she is saying?" "A lot, she has no reason to lie as far as I can tell. Also, there are whispers going around the station that a DS from this station is being investigated on corruption charges and putting two and two together, plus knowing what DS Jones is like personally, I believe he will try to tie up loose ends before he is possibly brought in for questioning sir." "Where are you now?" "I'm still up at the hospital sir," "Good, stay there.

I will call you back shortly." "Yes sir." DS Gregory hung up the phone, let out a sigh and for the first time in months he wished he had a cigarette.

Even though he was expecting his phone to ring, it still made him jump when it did ring. "DS Gregory." "Keith," the DI said, "I cannot confirm if anyone is being investigated by IPCC, but the ACC has suggested that I talk to the young lady before we set out to arrest DS Jones. Do we know of her current whereabouts?" "Yes sir, she is still here at the hospital." "Good make sure she stays there, and I will be with you within half an hour." "Sir, given the seriousness of the situation do you not think that SO19 should be deployed here, I would feel a lot happier if there was a little fire power here just in case the person or persons who killed Ben turn up here looking to tidy up another loose end." DI Jamerson thought about this for a minute and decided he would authorise an armed response unit attend the hospital. "Yes, I agree, I will get one on its way and inform them to liaise with you, any further developments call me immediately on my mobile." "Yes sir."

The armed response unit arrived at the hospital in less than 10 minutes, to the relief of DS Gregory, which made him feel more secure. "So, what gives Keith?" The armed officer asked. DS Gregory brought the armed unit up to speed on the murder but leaving out the information about DS Jones being a suspect, instead saying that no-one except himself or his DI were allowed anywhere near the office where the witness was being kept.

With the armed unit securing the corridor, DS Gregory went into the office and informed Carol that an armed unit were outside for her protection and that his boss was on his way to talk with her. "Has my son and mum been picked up yet?" Carol asked. "Yes, they have been taken to a place of safety by 2 female officers." "Thank you, that makes me feel a lot more comfortable."

DI Jamerson arrived at the hospital within 30 minutes, showing Carol his id, "hi, my name is Patrick Jamerson, I will be in charge of this case, DS Gregory has been keeping me updated, but I need to hear what has happened directly from you." Carol spent the next 10 minutes explaining how she first met the Police Officer called Jones, and how he went on to threaten both Ben and herself. "Can you give me a description of the person you call Jones?" After giving him the description, DI Jamerson asked he she would excuse him for a minute and signalled to DS Gregory to follow him out of the office.

"Well from the that description it sure sounds like David Jones, don't you agree Keith?" "I do, but what do we do now?" Just as he was finishing his reply, his phone chirped away in his pocket. Pulling it out looking at the screen it was showing that it was the comm's room, "Excuse me sir, but it's the comm's room, I need to take this," "go ahead." "DS Gregory," he answered, "Hi Keith, is Julie in comm's, just to give you an update, the car that was involved in this morning was stopped on the M4 outside Slough by a Royal Berks traffic unit. Two occupants were detained after a struggle, one of the occupants had blood splashes over his clothing and a machete with blood staining was found under the passenger seat." "Julie can you find out what station they have been taken to, phone them back and give them my number and inform whoever is in charge, that the prisoners will need an armed guard as a serving Police Officer may be involved and we don't want them to go missing or anything to happen to them." "Okay will do, anything else I can do for you honey?" "No thanks." He replied and disconnected the call. Turning back to the DI, "They have stopped the car involved in this morning's incident and captured 2 prisoners, one covered in blood and also recovered a blood-stained weapon." "Where are they being held?" "Not sure yet sir, but they were captured by the Royal Berk's on the M4, so I would guess it will be Reading Central." "Do we know if Jones was one of them?" "I will call Reading SCU and get more details sir." "Okay I will call Steve Munro in the drugs squad and find out what is going on down there." "Does that mean Jones IS being investigated sir?" he said with a cheeky smile. "I didn't say a word, did I. But there again I didn't deny it either did I." Keith Gregory just nodded complete with a knowing grin.

37

DI Jamerson, guided Carol out of this hospital into the back of an unmarked Police car. He got in beside her, "The plan is to take you home, so you can get an overnight bag together, we will then reunite you with your mum and son and then you will be taken to a safe location in Yorkshire until we can be certain it will be safe for you to return, you will be guarded at all times both inside and outside of the property. You will not be able to contact anyone by phone email or social media; this is for your own safety. Carol just sat there not saying a word as she desperately tried to come to terms with losing Ben and what was happening with her and her family.

After speaking with a DS from the Royal Berkshire Police Serious Crime Unit, DS Keith Gregory established that DS David Jones was not one of the suspects being held at Reading Central Police station. He arranged for them to be brought too closer to Swindon for questioning under a heavily armed guard.

A few hours later, the whole Serious Crime Unit were gathered in a meeting room in a local big chain hotel, as it was thought to be a safer option, so as no information could accidently escape.

DI Jamerson banged on the table to quieten the room, "Right people, let's get started. We have the two suspects being held at Hungerford Police Station. Both have been identified now, one is Cory Grey and the other is Titus Sanderson, both being known criminals from South London and both having links to the Yardies gangs in London and Bristol. What else have we got?" DS Gregory cleared his throat, "Well apart from the car the weapon and the suspects, that's it. I will be going off to interview the suspects with Hamilton as soon as we are finished here." "Well that's not a lot to be going on with," the DI said, "but what I am about to say does not leave this room. I have had it confirmed that Jones is being investigated by IPCC and he is at this time suspended from duty. One of the reasons he is suspended, is that he had been threatening both Ben Thorton and Carol Mcvitie. It does not take a genius to work out that he could well be involved in this murder, he may not have done it personally, but I'm damn sure he ordered it. So, team, find me the link and let's arrest this son of a bitch."

Cory Grey was brought out of his cell, dressed in what can best described as hospital scrubs, as all his own clothes had been taken away to be tested at the Police Lab in Surrey. The desk Sergeant informed him that he was going to be interviewed by two officers from Swindon and that a duty solicitor would be available if he required him, Cory indicated he did want the solicitor present.

Gregory and Hamilton entered the interview room at Hungerford Police Station, Gregory placed a cd in the recording machine and switched it on, then gave the date and time of the recording. He also checked that the video feed was being recorded as well.

"Cory Grey, my name is Detective Sergeant Gregory, I am from the Swindon Serious Crime Unit" "and I am Detective Constable Hamilton, also from Swindon Serious Crime Unit and also present is," pointing to the solicitor, "My name is Travis Jenkins and I am representing Cory Grey." "Right that's all the introductions done,

let's get down to why we are here. Cory can you confirm your full name and date of birth?" "No Comment!" Came the reply. "Cory all I'm asking you is to confirm you name and date of birth, I'm pretty certain you are not going to incriminate yourself by giving me those details," Once again the reply was "No Comment!" "Are you going to give 'No Comment to all the questions that we ask you?" "No Comment!" Was the reply. "Cory," it was Hamilton asking the questions now, "We have evidence placing you and Titus in Swindon at the scene of the murder of Ben Thorton. We also have the car which you were a passenger in at the time of being arrested, we also have what we believe to be the murder weapon, we also have your clothing which has blood splatters over it and I sure your DNA will be found on the victim and once all the evidence is put together you will be going to prison for a very long time. Make it easy on everyone and be sensible and talk to us." "No comment," replied Cory. "Okay Cory we will leave it there for the time being, but we will be interviewing you again shortly, so use that time to think about things and help us to help you." Gregory said.

After returning Cory to his cell, Gregory said "Let's grab a quick coffee before we talk to Titus and come up with a different plan to use on Titus." Hamilton agreed and said, "I suppose as the junior officer I have to pay for the coffee's," "of course but I tell you what if we get him to talk, I will buy you a steak meal on the way home." "You're on."

Ten minutes later, they were sat in the same interview room with Titus and with the same duty solicitor. But instead of a no comment interview that they were expecting, Titus started singing like the proverbial canary. Saying that they had gotten a message from a contact in the Metropolitan Police saying that they were wanted for a job in Swindon. They met the client at Membury Services, who gave them all the details of the person they were supposed to beat up. "So, you were not hired to kill the victim then?" Hamilton asked. "No just give him a good beating, but he started to fight back hard, that's when Cory went and got his machete and swung it wildly, he didn't mean to kill him just frighten him and we both just panicked and drove away." "How much were you going to get paid to do this?" Gregory asked. "£1500 up front and £1500 afterwards."

"How did you recognise the victim when you first saw him?" Gregory asked. "We were told that he would drop off his girlfriend at the hospital, we were then to take a picture of him and send it to a phone number we were given, once we had a message back confirming it was him we were to follow him and attack him when he got home or at a place which was quiet and there wasn't much chance of being seen." "And this is what you did?" "Yep." "Okay this interview is suspended while we go and check some details out." Gregory informed Titus and his solicitor. He ejected the cd and placed it in its box and he and the solicitor signed the seal.

Titus was taken back to his cell, "Any chance of a cup of coffee," Titus asked, "Yeah no problem, I will go and ask the Desk Sergeant to bring you one, how do you want it?" "White 2 sugars please."

"How's the interviewing of that prisoner going?" The desk Sergeant asked, "Very good," Gregory replied, "can you send him down a coffee white 2 sugars. Can you tell me was there a mobile phone in the prisoner's personal possessions?" "Let me just check." Punching down on the keyboard, the screen showed there were two mobiles taken off the prisoner's. "Can I have them please?" Gregory asked, "I would but they are still at Reading Central along with a large sum of money, I can give you the number of the Custody suite in Reading if you need it." "Yes please."

Leaving his DC to arrange for Royal Berks to bring the mobiles to Hungerford on the hurry up, Gregory made a call to his boss to give him an update. "I hope you are ringing to give me good news Keith!" "No and Yes" was the reply. "Don't fuck me around Keith, what is the situation, "Well Cory Grey gave a 'no comment' interview, that's the bad news but Titus Sanderson is talking like there is no tomorrow." "Excellent what is he saying?" Gregory went on to explain what Titus had said in his interview. "Brilliant we need to get those phones asap." "Already on it, Royal Berks are flying down the M4 with the phones as we speak. Any news on the whereabouts of Jones?" "Not yet, but we are working on it, but trying to keep it on the 'QT' is making life a lot harder." "I bet it is." "As soon as you have any definite proof Jones is involved call me then we will go live with an arrest warrant for Jones." "Yes, sir hopefully it won't be too long."

Gregory found Hamilton in the Police canteen tucking into a sausage sandwich, "So where the hell is my sandwich?" he asked "Dunno Sarge, wasn't sure what you wanted, and I couldn't ask you as you were busy on the phone chatting away to the chief." Hamilton laughed. "Anymore of that and you will be directing traffic for the rest of your miserable career."

38

24 hours later, the whole of the SCU reconvened, but this time at Swindon Police Station. "Right then folks," DCI Jamerson started, "Things have moved forward quite a lot over the last 24 hours, firstly David Jones was positively identified by Carol Mcvitie and also Titus Sanderson. We have had the suspects phone analysed and we can confirm that the suspects did contact Jones on his own mobile phone and that Jones messaged them back, informing them that it was Ben Thorton in the picture and to go ahead with the attack. We have also received statements from various witnesses alleging that Jones was demanding money off them in return for not being arrested on drugs charges. We also have statements from female witnesses who claim that he insisted on them committing sexual acts, once again for not being charged on drugs charges. There are at the moment 2 allegations of rape against Jones. I have been speaking with the investigation officer at IPCC and he has agreed to put his

investigation on the back burner while we put a case together against Jones. I have spoken to the suits upstairs and we have the go ahead to find and arrest Jones." "Have we any idea were Jones is?" Hamilton asked the group. They all shook their heads. "I want you all out on the streets, using all your contacts to find this son of a bitch. It will be announced at the start of all shifts, that there is a warrant out for his arrest."

The news of the arrest warrant was the talk of the Police Station and it soon became clear just how unliked Jones really was. People were popping their heads into the SCU's office suggesting possible places where he might be found. It was just after 2pm when the news of a confirmed sighting of Jones in a local coffee shop was passed onto the SCU.

An armed response unit was sent to the scene, where Jones was arrested without an incident and brought into Swindon Police station. Even though he knew it was breaking all the rules Keith Gregory couldn't help himself, he went down to the cells, he opened the observation hatch and looked into the cell at Jones.

"What the fuck do you want you fucking poofter." "Oh, how the mighty have fallen, you homophobic wanker, you are going down for a very long time, and when they find out you're an ex-copper and believe me I will make sure they do find out, your life will be hell and I will love every minute of it." "Go and fuck yourself." "Well that will be so much better than being some horny 20 stone hairy assed prisoners bitch." With that he slammed the hatch shut and walked away. Stopping off at the Custody's Sergeant's desk, "I have just informed the prisoner that we won't be interviewing him until tomorrow morning Sarge." "I bet that not all you said." The custody Sergeant said with a big smile on his face.

In the early hours of the next morning, Keith Gregory was awoken by the sound of his phone ringing. "Gregory," "Morning Keith, it's Pete in the custody suite. Sorry to call you this early in the morning Keith but we have a problem here, when we did our routine cell check, we found Jones hanging in his cell. We cut him down, but he was pronounced dead by the duty doctor." "The fucking coward why was he not watched?" "He wasn't on our suicide watch list."

"How the hell did he do it?" "He ripped his top into strips, tied them all together, looped it over the camera cage." "The shit is really going to hit the fan in the morning Pete.

Has my DI been informed yet?" "There was no answer from his phones, both home and mobile. You were next on the list, that's why I called you." "There is no point in me coming now, but I will make sure that I'm in before he gets in." "Okay Keith I will see you shortly."

The shit really did hit the fan, when the top brass started to arrive in the morning and learnt of Jones suicide. DI Jamerson's face was purple with anger, "We work like demented chickens to put a solid case together and they let him hang himself, somebodies head is going to roll for this." A few minutes later after a coffee to calm himself down, he announced to the squad, "but on the plus side, we won't have to drag the force through the mud and expose the ugly corrupt under belly of a few officers." "I agree sir," Keith Gregory said, "and we will continue to weed them out and bring back the respect of the public in the process sir."

Epilogue

6 Months Later

The Coroner's inquest into Tina Williamson's death resulted in an open verdict as there was not enough evidence to prove that she was murdered. The police will keep her file open and marked unsolved.

The Coroner's inquest into Ben Thornton's ruled that his death was a case of unlawful killing. Titus Sanderson, carried on helping the Police, telling them all about the yardies criminal activities in and around London and about who in the Met they had dealings with. After being promised a lighter sentence, when he finally went to court. At court he was imprisoned for10 years. Cory Grey continued to plead his innocence even when shown all the evidence the Police had against him. At Bristol Crown Court he was sentenced to life in prison and was told he would serve a minimum of 25 years.

The Coroner's inquest into DS David Jones was ruled as a suicide. Following an internal investigation by the Avon and Somerset Police Force, one other officer from the drug squad was found to be taking bribes in return for turning a blind eye to certain drug dealer's activities. He was arrested and sentenced to 3 years in prison. David Jones family's rights to his pension were refused.

Ben Thornton's funeral was paid for by the Department for Work and Pensions, only 1 person attended. His mum

On hearing about the suspicion of Ben's involvement in Tina Williamson's death, Carol Mcvitie decided not to attend his funeral but to put the whole sorry affair behind her. She also transferred out of the A&E dept and moved to the operating theatres as a scrub nurse. Where she met and started dating a fellow scrub nurse called Nick.

For all his hard work and dedication DS
Keith Gregory was promoted to Detective
Inspector.

Printed in Great Britain
by Amazon